'I'm sorry, Lo

'What for?'

'For dragging you into this mess.'

'You didn't drag me and we still don't know what sort of mess it is.' He gathered her into his arms and pressed his lips to hers. 'I'm sure whatever it is you'll meet it head-on and triumph.'

'How do you know?'

'Because you have an honest heart. Regardless of the fact that you can't remember who you are or who's after you, you're honest, Charli, and you need to hold firm to that. Trust your instincts, just as you've been doing, and you won't go wrong.'

Lucy Clark began writing romance in her early teens and immediately knew she'd found her 'calling' in life. After working as a secretary in a busy teaching hospital, she turned her hand to writing medical romance. She currently lives in South Australia with her husband and two children. Lucy largely credits her writing success to the support of her husband, family and friends.

Recent titles by the same author:

THE ENGLISH DOCTOR'S DILEMMA
HIS PREGNANT GP
THE REGISTRAR'S WEDDING WISH

DIAGNOSIS: AMNESIA

BY
LUCY CLARK

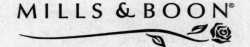

MILLS & BOON®

To Melanie & Austin
You are both such perfect gifts of love.
Love always, Mummy
Ps 115:1

MILLS & BOON and MILLS & BOON with the Rose Device are registered trademarks of the publisher.

*First published in Great Britain 2004
Harlequin Mills & Boon Limited,
Eton House, 18-24 Paradise Road, Richmond, Surrey TW9 1SR*

© Lucy Clark 2004

ISBN 0 263 83926 5

*Set in Times Roman 10 on 10½ pt.
03-1004-57022*

*Printed and bound in Spain
by Litografia Rosés, S.A., Barcelona*

PROLOGUE

'IT'S not *that* bad, Charlotte.'

Charli turned and looked at Chuck in surprise. 'But what you're asking me to do is…is unethical. I can't do that, I just can't.'

Charli allowed Chuck to steer her down the hotel corridor towards the lift. He pressed the button and pointed to her hair. 'You'd better check that. I think you have a few strands loose.'

Charli immediately checked her chignon but it felt fine. Still, she smoothed fingers along her hair before running a hand down her beige skirt, making sure that was straight and in place. She buttoned her matching jacket and glanced at the man before her. 'Better?'

He gave her a quick appraisal. 'I guess.'

Charli frowned. 'You seem a little agitated. What have I done wrong?'

'You're not agreeing to what I need you to do, Charlotte. I could lose my job if you don't change your research findings. You wouldn't want that to happen, would you?'

'No, of course not.' He was acting a little strange and she wasn't quite sure why.

'I didn't think you would. So you'll do it?' He reached out his hand to her, his fingers scooping up the gold necklace which hung around her neck. The chain held a love-heart pendant which had been engraved on the back with 'Love, Chuck'. 'For me?'

His gaze held hers and Charli could feel herself wilting. She hated it when he looked at her like that because it made her feel guilty. He'd always been so nice to her, ever since they'd met, and just before they'd left for this trip to Australia he'd given her the necklace. Charli had been overjoyed at the sentiment, even though the style of the piece didn't really suit her. She edged back slightly and he dropped his hand.

5

'I can't, Chuck. I'm sorry.' She watched as his eyes clouded over and quickly continued, 'Didn't you read my report?' She shook her head, puzzled. 'Perhaps you didn't understand it properly.'

'Don't pull that genius routine with me.' His tone was rough and she widened her eyes in disbelief.

'Chuck?'

'You may be a genius but don't make me out to be an idiot, honey, because I'm not. You don't have the first clue what's been going on here, do you?'

She dragged a breath into her lungs which felt as though they were going to compress. 'Why don't you tell me?' she said flatly, her words a little shaky.

'It's simple. I need you to report the results I tell you to report at the international medical conference next week. That's all you have to do, Charli.' He ran his finger lightly down her cheek in a caress that made her feel sick. It surprised her. Chuck had always been so kind and gentle. What was wrong with him today?

She turned away from his touch and pressed the lift-call button again for something to do. 'These elevators take for ever,' she mumbled, wanting to get out of this hallway. Chuck's words had unnerved her and right now it was the last thing she needed. She had to focus. She was about to give another lecture at the small Australian medical conference when in reality all she wanted to do was to return to LA where she felt safe.

Why had she let Chuck talk her into coming to Australia in the first place? It had been the pharmaceutical company's idea, and the fact that they were paying for her entire trip had been an incentive. When Charli had asked Chuck why they wanted her to go to Australia, he had said it was to raise awareness for her research. He'd managed to talk her around, promising to be there by her side and then suggesting they take a little time afterwards and spend a few days at Queensland's Great Barrier Reef.

'I'll take care of everything,' Chuck had said over dinner.

'You just need to worry about being gorgeous and brilliant, which isn't hard for you.'

Charli had been flattered by his words and had agreed to go. Chuck had always been gentle and attentive during the time they'd spent together. For the first time in her life, she felt as though she'd met a man who hadn't resented her work, who'd been supportive and who had actually cared for her. He'd sent her flowers, he'd wined and dined her and Charli had been swept off her feet and caught up in the romantic schoolgirl notions she'd never had the opportunity to explore before.

Now she was wondering whether she'd made a big mistake. Not in attending the conference but in believing Chuck when he'd said he'd take care of everything. Did *everything* include her doing exactly what the pharmaceutical company wanted? What would happen if she stood her ground and refused to falsify her results?

Charli began to worry, biting her lower lip in concern. All she wanted to do right now was to get home as soon as possible, back to her comfort zones. There were only two places where she felt completely comfortable and that was when she was consulting with her patients or in her laboratory, doing research.

Finally, the elevator arrived and she stepped in, hoping someone else would join them. No one did. Chuck was right behind her and she pressed the button for level two where the conference was being held before darting a look at him. 'Chuck. I know how important your job is to you but, honestly, I can't present false results to an international conference.' Her voice was quiet yet matter-of-fact, hoping she could see him make sense. 'I am a leading voice in the medical and biomedical research world, not to mention the head of unit at the largest teaching hospital in Los Angeles. People listen to my opinions, they respect my expertise on these subjects. To lie to them would be…well, it would be wrong.'

Chuck shifted uneasily and clenched his hands into fists. 'No. You don't understand, Charlotte. You *must* do this. It isn't open to negotiation and, besides, the company will take good care of you.'

She looked up at him and was alarmed to find his smoky grey eyes as dark as storm clouds. He reached out and gripped her arm, causing her earlier worry to intensify.

'Chuck? You're hurting me.' Fear seized her and for a moment she found it difficult to breathe.

'Billions of dollars are at stake here, Charlotte. You don't seem to understand that either.' He let go of her arm and took a step away, as though just the thought of touching her repulsed him.

'But if I falsify my results and endorse it the way you want, babies may *die*. The product from your pharmaceutical company causes *cancer*, Chuck. Didn't you read my report?'

'Your report is worthless. A new report is being prepared for you.'

'You can't do that.'

'Watch me.'

The lift doors opened and, feeling ill, Charli stumbled out and rushed to the ladies' bathroom. She went into a cubicle and sat down, desperately trying to get control of herself. She was trembling all over and as she felt a tear drift off her lashes and trickle down her cheek, she began to feel dizzy.

'Breathe, breathe.' She said the word slowly, over and over forcing herself to take deep, calming breaths. 'You'll figure this out. You'll be fine.' Even as she said the words, she couldn't possibly see how she could be. She was trapped. Trapped in Australia with Chuck. Was that the reason he'd brought her here? Why the company had paid all her expenses? If she didn't do what they wanted, were they planning to just leave her here so she would miss the international conference?

Desperation gripped Charli's heart as she recalled the look of revulsion Chuck had given her. It made her want to ask him about their own relationship. What exactly did she mean to him? At the moment, it was hard to believe he'd ever really cared about her at all!

She blew her nose and worked harder to get herself under

control. She was supposed to be speaking to a roomful of delegates in approximately three minutes and all she wanted to do was to sob her heart out as she'd never done before. She might be a highly intelligent woman where it came to her work, but in affairs of the heart she was a novice.

Charli hiccuped and bit her lip. How had things turned out so bad? What was she supposed to do now? Dragging a deep breath into her lungs, she knew she needed a plan of action. There were only a few hours of the conference left and then she could leave. Where would she go? Chuck had her passport and the airplane tickets. Could she find them? Sneak into his room and get them back?

She needed money. She could probably ring the airline and change her ticket so she could fly back tomorrow but then Chuck would be right behind her, hard on her heels. 'Oh, think,' she muttered to herself as she went to splash some water on her face. She eyed her reflection, glad her nose or eyes hadn't puffed up too much.

Taking the make-up compact from her jacket pocket, she powdered her nose. Then she slipped the pendant beneath her shirt where she couldn't see it. She needed to focus. 'You'll be fine.' This time when she said the words, she began to feel them. 'You'll work it out.'

What she needed was to hole up in her laboratory for a few days, put on some Tchaikovsky and think everything through. As that option was unavailable, she wondered whether she could get away for a few days here in Australia. Yes...but not where Chuck had planned. She'd already cleared her work schedule and the hospital wasn't expecting her back until just before the international conference to be held Wednesday next week.

Where she would go was anyone's guess. At least, for the moment, she had a plan and that was enough to help get her mind back on track. She looked at her reflection, checking her blonde chignon once more. Smoothing her hand down her suit, she nodded. 'You're a professional and a grown woman.' Her words were spoken sternly and she looked at herself critically.

Her professional mask was back in place and after taking another deep breath, she felt much better.

The instant she stepped out of the ladies' room, her assistant came up and gave her the notes for her next lecture.

'You're in the main lecture room—where you were this morning,' he said.

'Thank you,' she said absent-mindedly as she glanced around the room but, thankfully, there was no sign of Chuck. 'Just give me a moment to review them.'

Across the room, Logan watched her smile politely at the people still milling around outside the lecture hall as she made her way to the far corner. She kept glancing around the room and he wondered if she was looking for someone in particular. Her back was ramrod straight, her chin held firm with a hint of defiance, and from what he'd seen of her that weekend, her ice-blue gaze could cut a man in two with a simple look. Her whole body language screamed, Leave me alone, and that was enough to intrigue him.

'Daddy? Are you listening to me?'

'Yes, Trin. Of course I am. Tell Grandma I'll probably be going straight to the hospital once I'm finished here.'

'So I won't see you until the morning?'

He smiled at the disappointment in his daughter's voice. 'I promise to come and give you a kiss when I get home.'

'All right. I have to go. Grandma says it's almost time for a bath. Do I have to have a bath, Dad? Can't I have a shower?'

'You can have a shower but don't get your hair wet.'

'Yay. OK. See you when you kiss me, Daddy. Love you.'

'Love you, too, princess.' Logan rang off, the smile still on his face as he switched his cellphone to silent and put it in his jacket pocket. Another man, also speaking on a cellphone, accidentally nudged him as he passed by. Logan murmured a polite 'Sorry' but the man ignored him.

'No. She'll play ball. I have her at my beck and call.' He paused. 'Well, if she *does* refuse, then I'll have to switch to more drastic measures.' Another pause. 'Simple. I know her mother. If she thinks her mother's life is in danger, she'll do whatever we like. So we just send her mother out of town for a few days and let her think something bad has happened. All she'll get is an answering machine and that should be enough to do the trick.' The man paused again. 'Don't worry about it. I'll take care of it.'

Logan picked up his conference folder which was full of the notes he'd taken during Charli Summerfield's lectures, trying hard not to eavesdrop on the other man's conversation. He had no idea who the man was or who he was talking to but, whoever he was talking about, it didn't sound good. Logan walked away and then turned to get a good look at the man. American accent, blonde hair, thinning slightly on top, grey eyes and dressed in a pinstripe suit. He'd seen him around the conference during the weekend but that was all.

'Excuse me, Doctor, the lecture is about to start,' a hotel official told him.

'Thank you.' Logan headed over to the door where a group of people had gathered. In the centre was Dr Summerfield herself. He paused, taking his first real opportunity to study her at close quarters.

She had her polite 'keep your distance' smile in place, her hand gripping her notes with repressed frustration.

As she edged away, another man stopped her and furiously pumped her hand, but it was the man standing directly behind him who caught her eye. She glanced at him, trying to focus on what the other person was saying. She smiled and murmured a polite reply then turned her attention to the man behind him.

'Logan Hargraves.' His voice was as smooth as silk and it washed over her in a wave of satisfaction. His blue gaze pierced right through to her soul as though he could see every secret she'd hidden deep inside. He extended his hand and she put hers forward, surprised at the tingles which spread up her arm the instant they made contact. She gave a firm but polite squeeze and glanced away, her gaze clashing with Chuck's. He was standing off to the side and she realised he wanted to speak to her again. Well, she wasn't in the mood just now. She held onto Dr Hargraves's hand and urged him a little closer to the lecture hall.

He was momentarily confused as Dr Summerfield almost tugged him into the doorway of the lecture hall. 'It's a...a pleasure to meet you.'

'Thank you.' She glanced over his shoulder to where Chuck stood. 'Uh...where are you from?'

The question caught him off guard. It was as though something had spooked her, and although he desperately wanted to glance over his shoulder to see who she'd just looked at, he resisted the urge. Instead, he concentrated on the woman before him. She'd gone from cool, calm and definitely sophisticated to being as skittish as a ring-tailed possum in a steam-roller factory.

'Er...I live in Halls Gap. It's about two hours' drive from here in the heart of the Grampians mountain range.'

'Small town?'

'Small enough.'

'So you're the GP there?'

'That's right. I also have a diploma in emergency medicine and do a stint at Stawell Hospital, which isn't far from where I live. I've found your lectures to be very informative but I'm sure that's what everyone's saying.' The smile reached his eyes as he spoke and Chuck was instantly forgotten. Logan's blue depths came to life in such a way that Charli felt herself totally mesmerised.

'You're the doctor who presented the paper first thing yesterday morning.' She nodded, her opinion of him growing. 'You raised some interesting points.'

'Er...thank you. I had no idea you were in the room.' She was still holding his hand and as they'd talked, they'd progressed from being at the back of the lecture hall, making their way towards the stairs. Logan glanced down at their hands and Charli instantly let go.

'Oh, I'm so sorry. I forgot.'

He raised an enquiring eyebrow. 'Forgot you were holding my hand?' He became even more intrigued by her as a blush gently touched her cheeks.

'I'm purported to be a genius, Dr Hargraves, and as such am known to be a little...absent-minded at times.'

A slow and very sexy smile spread across his face, his blue eyes twinkling. 'How lucky for you to have a good excuse.'

Charli felt her knees weaken and butterflies take flight in her stomach. Good heavens! She was attracted to this man. She didn't know him from Adam and yet she felt a connection…a bond…and she'd never felt anything like that in her life.

Her assistant touched her arm, telling her it was time to go. Charli nodded and turned back to Logan.

Her heart was hammering wildly with unrepressed excitement as she looked into his eyes. She wanted to see him again. Should she ask him out?

She stepped a little closer and cleared her throat. 'Perhaps we can…' She couldn't believe she was saying this '…catch up some time. You know, to discuss your paper. There were some points you could expand on a little.' Oh, her words sounded so lame but she quickly rushed on before she ran out of courage. 'My schedule's pretty tight but…perhaps drinks after the proceedings finish tonight?' Good. That would also give her an excuse to avoid Chuck.

The look he gave her was totally encompassing and she reached out a hand to the wall to steady herself.

'You have no idea how much I'd like that…but I have to leave directly after your lecture and won't be here at the end of the day.' He seemed as disappointed as she suddenly felt. 'I'm sorry.' He shrugged. 'I have to work tonight but if you have a few days before you fly back to America, perhaps you'd consider coming to visit the famous Grampians. There are some great walks we could go on.'

Charli shifted backwards and nodded, her mind working furiously. 'You know, that's not such a bad idea.' Her assistant touched her arm again, urging her to move. 'I'll give that some thought.' She extended her hand again, eager to touch him once more. 'It was a pleasure to meet you, Logan.'

He took her hand in his and raised it to his lips, his gaze never leaving hers. 'Likewise…Charli.'

CHAPTER ONE

'HELLO?' Years of being instantly awake when a phone rang worked on Logan Hargraves once more as he struggled to clear his mind from sleep.

'Logan. It's Wil. I need you. I'll be around to pick you up in ten minutes.'

'OK.' Logan replaced the phone, turned to look at the digital read-out of the clock and then dropped back onto the pillows when he realised it was just before six o'clock in the morning.

'Dad?' The little voice from the door made him raise his head once more. Two pairs of brown eyes stared back at him.

'You're both awake early.' He returned his head to the pillows and motioned for them to come in.

'We heard the phone,' Trinity said as she climbed into bed beside him and snuggled in.

'I was already awake,' Owen declared as he bounded onto the bed, making Logan groan in pain. He reached up and wrestled his son down for a morning cuddle.

'Well, I was sound asleep and snoring my head off,' Logan said, his words making both of them giggle.

'You're a loud snorer, Daddy,' Owen stated.

'Uh-uh. You're louder, Owen,' Trinity said, not missing the opportunity to bait her younger brother.

'Am not.'

'Are, too.'

'Am not.'

'Not this early,' Logan groaned, more to himself than the two children who were messing up his nice warm bed. 'It's time to get up.'

'No.' Both of them protested, their earlier disagreement instantly forgotten.

'You need to get dressed for school and then off to

14

Grandma's for breakfast. That was Wil on the phone. He's going to be here soon.'

'Has there been an accident?' Owen asked.

'I think so. Wil will tell me the details when he picks me up. Right now I need to get dressed, get some medical supplies and get you two to Grandma's house.' Logan sat up, pulling the blankets with him.

'Don't, Daddy. I'm cold,' Trinity complained.

'Then get dressed,' he said as he stumbled from the bed, his foot getting caught in the sheets. Logan shooed them out of his room and quickly changed into a pair of jeans and a shirt before pulling on his socks and boots. Next, he gave his mother a quick call to let her know of the emergency. 'It's a cold one,' he mumbled as he headed to the coatrack to find his jacket. 'Make sure you put your jackets on.'

'But, Dad,' Owen protested, 'it's warm at lunchtime.'

'I know but it's cold now. Grab your schoolbag. Come on, Trin,' he called. 'Time to go.'

'I'm coming, I'm coming,' she said with the perfect feminine impatience of a seven-year-old. 'I don't like being rushed in the mornings.'

'Believe me, sweetheart, neither do I.' Logan held the front door open for his children as a police car pulled up. He quickly ushered the kids across the street to his mother's house. 'Give me a sec, Wil. I still need to stop by the clinic.'

Logan returned two minutes later and headed to the surgery which was next door to his home. Wil fell into step beside him. 'What's the deal?'

'Craig took a tourist party out hiking about half an hour ago. They found a woman near the Venus Baths. Looks as though she's fallen down a small ravine.'

'Dead or alive?' Logan unlocked the door and headed down the corridor to the back room. He picked up a backpack and began putting supplies in while Wil talked.

'Alive for the moment. Craig abseiled down to check her out and has covered her with a blanket as he said she was extremely cold. She's still unconscious.'

'You've spoken to Craig?'

'No. This report is from the hikers. They returned to raise the alarm. We'll need to hoist her out on a stretcher. I've already called for the ambulance.'

'I wonder how long she's been there.'

'Your guess is as good as mine, mate.'

Logan finished his packing and walked back down the corridor. 'It was pretty cold last night. Well, the sooner we get to her the sooner we'll find out.' Logan locked his surgery door and headed over to the waiting police car. He looked up at his mother's house and saw Owen's face pressed against the window. He waved to him as they pulled away.

'He's looking more and more like his dad every day.' Wil shook his head in wonderment. 'Hard to believe it's almost five years since Trevor and Alison died.'

'Time doesn't stop. Life goes on and the pain takes a long time to fade.'

'Some days I still find it hard to believe you gave up a lucrative Toorak practice to move back here to be with your brother's kids.'

'There was nothing else to do,' Logan told his friend. 'And I wouldn't change it for the world. Those kids…they're wonderful. Some days I wish they really were mine.'

'They are, mate. Legally and emotionally. You're their dad.'

'Yeah.' Logan knew now was not the time to dwell on things. He needed to focus on the rescue they were about to do. The woman would no doubt be suffering from hypothermia, depending on how long she'd been out there. Fractures, sprains, bruises—they might all be present.

'Did she have any identification on her?' he asked.

'Craig couldn't find any.' Wil parked the car and then started to unload the equipment they'd need. Logan put his backpack on and took the portable stretcher while Wil loaded himself up with the satellite phone, more blankets, ropes and other things which he put into his own backpack. 'Let's go.'

They started walking and soon came to the Venus Baths. It was a slightly rocky and uneven area where tourists could come and relax amongst the slow-running pools of water. They kept going, heading towards the end where large rocks blocked off a path. They climbed over, carefully lifting the equipment, and continued down the path.

'Craig?' Logan called out.

'Down here,' Craig called back. 'Took your time,' he joked.

'It was Logan's fault. Had to kiss his kids,' Wil added as he took the backpack off. Logan did the same and looked down the small embankment to where Craig was lying beside a woman, sharing his body warmth.

'How is she?'

'Still very cold.'

'What's the best way down?'

'You'd be best to abseil. We're on a bit of a slope and I wouldn't want you to fall, mate.'

'You're the expert.' Logan waited for Wil to pass him a harness. Soon the rope was down and Logan was ready. 'Once I'm down, send the backpack and then the stretcher,' he told Wil.

'Right.'

Abseiling and rock-climbing had never been a favourite pastime of Logan's but since his arrival in Halls Gap five years ago, it was something he'd become proficient at. Unlike Craig, he didn't choose to spend his leisure time clambering around on cliffs.

Once he was down, he stayed attached to the rope but locked himself in. 'Whoa. This ravine is steeper than I thought. You make it look so calm and natural, Craig.' Logan pulled off his thick gloves and tucked them into the back pocket of his jeans before retrieving the medical torch from his jacket.

'That's my job,' Craig replied. 'Rig up another rope,' he called to Wil.

Logan left the technicalities to Wil and Craig and concentrated on his patient. Her blonde hair was messy and half over her face, and her clothing was intact. Her pupils were equal and reacting to light, which was a good sign. 'Miss? Miss? Can you hear me? My name is Logan. Miss?'

No response.

Logan brushed the hair from her face and gasped as recognition dawned on him. 'I know her.' He ignored the stirring in his gut. He'd experienced the same feeling the first time he'd laid eyes on her at the conference. Dr Charlotte Summerfield was an amazingly good-looking woman. Although his love life had been non-existent for the past five years, there was nothing wrong with his hormones, especially when it came to admiring the natural beauty of such a stunning woman.

'You do?' Craig seemed surprised. 'You know her?'

'Yeah. She was the guest speaker at the medical conference I went to in Melbourne last weekend. Charli Summerfield.'

'Charlie?'

'Short for Charlotte but Charli—with no "e"—was the name on her badge at the conference, so I guess that's what she prefers to be called.' Logan checked her pulse while he spoke. 'Skin's very cool. Pulse is down but that's to be expected and she's still shivering. That's a good sign, means her body temperature hasn't dropped below 31°C.'

'Hypothermia?'

'Yes.' He ran his hands over her skull and discovered a contusion at the back. 'She's hit her head at least twice, so between that and the hypothermia it's no wonder she's unconscious.' He put the Timpani thermometer in her ear. '33.6°C. We need to get her out of here, stat.' Next, he pulled a pair of heavy duty scissors from his backpack and began cutting away her clothes. 'Keep that blanket around her as best you can,' he instructed Craig. When he'd dealt with her clothes, he checked her for fractured bones but thankfully everything felt fine. Both men were as close to her as possible, continuing to share their body warmth. Logan took her blood pressure. 'It's low. Not too far but we need to move fast.' He listened to her chest. It was a bit tight but, again, that was to be expected.

Wil was getting the stretcher set up as Logan pulled out a cervical collar and placed it carefully around her neck. 'How's the stretcher coming, Wil?'

'Almost there. Just getting ready to send it down now.'

'Good.'

Wil sent the stretcher down, tied to the rope that he and

Craig had secured. Craig grabbed the stretcher and together Logan worked with him to secure Charli in place. Craig secured the straps and hooked the stretcher back up to the ropes so they could pull her up to safety.

'I'll go on up and you stay down here and come up with her,' Craig said, and Logan nodded his agreement. 'You'll be all right climbing up, won't you?'

'I guess.' He grinned at his friend. 'Lucky I brought my gloves.' Logan retrieved them and pulled them on as Craig started to scale the ravine with complete ease, taking Logan's backpack with him. Once he was at the top, they were ready. Wil and Craig pulled on the ropes and the stretcher slowly rose. Logan watched Charli closely, praying she wouldn't choose this moment to regain consciousness.

He tried to keep up with the stretcher but it was impossible. When she was almost up to the top, he began concentrating on his own climb, using the rope to pull himself up. He was nearly at the top when Craig called down that he'd give him a hand, and a moment later Logan felt himself being hauled upwards.

'Thanks.' He smiled at his mate before turning his attention to Charli. Ripping off his gloves, he reached for the backpack once more and checked her obs.

'BP's still low, pupils are fine. Temperature, respiratory rate—both low.'

'Overnight stay?' Wil asked.

'At the least. It depends on what other injuries we can find, but just by running my hands over her bones, I couldn't feel any breaks. The longer she stays unconscious, the worse the outcome might be.' Logan zipped up his backpack, slung it onto his back and nodded to his two friends. 'Let's get her out of here.'

They started the journey back towards the parking area, and the ambulance was waiting for them by the time they arrived. He climbed in beside her after she'd been transferred to the stretcher. 'Charli?' He called again. 'Charli? Can you hear me?' Still no response. He looked at her face. She was quite pale although her body temperature was slowly increasing, which was a good sign.

She wore a gold chain around her neck as well as earrings, and Logan carefully removed them, checking her wrists, ankles and fingers for other jewellery before sealing them in a plastic bag. Next, Logan set up a saline drip and placed the oxygen mask over her mouth and nose.

'Charli?' he said again as the ambulance got under way. 'My name is Logan Hargraves. I'm a doctor. We're taking you to hospital.'

'Hospital?'

Had he imagined it or had she mumbled the word?

'Charli? Can you hear me?'

'No need to yell,' she grumbled, frowning. She tried to raise her hand to her face but couldn't because she was strapped in.

'Don't move.' Logan lowered his voice but kept it firm and direct. 'You've hit your head and were unconscious.'

'You're a paramedic?' she asked, her American twang sliding out.

'Doctor. My name is Logan Hargraves. We met briefly the other day at the medical conference in Melbourne. Today, though, you're not in such great shape. You've had an accident and hit your head. You have a medial and lateral contusion of your skull but thankfully no fractured bones. You'll need X-rays on arrival and I'd like you to be kept overnight for observation. The usual,' he said with a mild shrug. While he spoke, he performed her obs once more. She was silent and he wondered if she'd drifted off once more. 'Charli? Can you open your eyes for me?'

She tried hard and eventually was able to open them, but only just.

'Good. How many fingers am I holding up?'

'Two.'

'Good.'

She closed her eyes again.

'Do you remember what happened?' He fastened the cuff around her arm and took her blood pressure, watching her closely. He received no response. 'Dr Summerfield? Charli? Can you hear me?'

'Yes, and I wish you'd stop yelling.'

'Do you have a headache?' He knew she must but he needed her to be conscious of the pain.

'What do you think? Of course I do.'

He smiled. 'A grumpy patient is much better than a silent one.' The ambulance was slowing down. 'Looks like we're at your stop. How's the pain?'

'Not good.'

'I'll give you something once we're inside.'

The doors opened and they were met by an orderly who helped get the stretcher out of the ambulance and wheeled it into the hospital. 'Dr Charli Summerfield,' Logan reported. 'Thirty-one years old, visiting Australia from America.' He gave the brief of where she'd been found and wrote up the tests he wanted. 'She needs to have a chest X-ray to check for pulmonary oedema as well as aspiration pneumonia. ECG as well. For her head injury, I want X-rays of the spine and skull and, depending on what they show, possibly a CT scan as well.

'Blood test—cross-type and match; arterial blood gas; electrolyte and glucose levels,' he told Maree, the sister on duty. 'Urine test for myoglobin, creatinine, blood urea nitrogen and amylase. Get a cardiac monitor in here so we can keep a watch on her heart. Obs every fifteen minutes. We have no idea how long she was unconscious, or how long she'd been lying there in the cold. Temperature is slowly rising.'

'Yes, Logan,' Maree replied as Charli was transferred to a hospital bed.

Now that she wasn't constricted by the ambulance stretcher anymore, Charli slowly raised a shaky hand to her head, feeling for herself the bumps the doctor called Logan had mentioned. Sure enough, there they were and she had one of those horrible collars around her throat. She'd worn one when she'd fallen from her horse when she'd been fifteen and she hadn't liked it then. She shivered a little and the nurse helped her get her hand beneath the blanket once more.

'As soon as we've eliminated the possibility of a spinal

injury, that collar can come off,' Logan said, and she realised he'd been watching her. 'When I checked you out before, I couldn't feel any fractures but that's what the X-rays will confirm.'

Charli moved her gaze to connect with his, keeping her head as still as possible. 'So you checked me out, did you?' Her voice echoed a little beneath the mask.

Logan smiled at her. 'You know perfectly well what I meant, Dr Summerfield.'

'What about the oxygen mask? When can that come off?'

'When I'm satisfied with your oxygen levels, Doctor, as you should well know.' His blue eyes twinkled with repressed mirth.

Charli closed her eyes and tried to relax. Who was this man and why did his smile seem to upset her heart rate so much? She could feel it pounding wildly beneath her ribs, and until a few moments ago it had been quite steady. Perhaps it was his Australian accent. Had she hired an Australian to work in her unit? She couldn't remember. Either way, she hoped he wasn't a troublemaker because it was the last thing she needed right now. There was too much pressure in her life already and she didn't need any more.

'Now, I believe something for the pain was in order before we got out of the ambulance.' He was writing on her chart as he spoke. 'Allergic to anything?'

Charli opened her eyes and thought—and then thought hard. Was she allergic to anything? She couldn't remember. If she'd been wearing an Alert bracelet, he would have already seen it and noted the details. She cleared her throat. 'Not that I know of.'

'I'll give you codeine phosphate but let me know if it doesn't work.' He drew up the injection and administered it via the drip. 'That should start working soon. When you're out of X-ray, the police will be wanting a word with you. Let me know if you're not feeling up to it and we can reschedule for tomorrow.'

'Tomorrow?' Charli frowned. 'What's happening tomorrow?'

Logan smiled again, although this time it was a more cautious smile mixed with concern. 'For you—nothing. You're staying in overnight and we'll decide tomorrow what happens next.'

Alarm ripped through Charli. She couldn't stay here overnight. She had no idea why but she just knew she couldn't stay here. Besides, she was a senior staff member at this hospital and had the right to pull a string or two to get herself discharged. If this man thought she was going to stay, he had another think coming. She struggled to move but the nurse gently stopped her. Charli's frustration grew.

'I won't be staying, Dr Hargraves, so don't bother filling in the forms. I'll have a word with Manny and he'll sort this thing out for me.'

'Manny? Who's Manny?'

'He's the CEO of the hospital.'

'Manny? Sorry. I don't know anyone by that name.'

'He would have hired you. He approves all senior staff, which I presume you are because you're treating me.'

Logan watched his patient closely. 'Which hospital is that, Dr Summerfield?'

'Why…' Charli stopped. What *was* the name of the hospital? Oh, it was so ridiculous. She'd been working there since her graduation over ten years ago. It was then she decided that perhaps Dr Hargraves was having a little joke at her expense. 'Stop being a pain. You know very well what the name of this hospital is.'

'I do. It's Stawell Hospital.'

'Stawell?' That wasn't right.

'Stawell Hospital in Victoria.' Again, Logan watched her closely. 'Australia.'

'*Australia?* What am I doing in Australia?'

'Hmm.' He could see the panic in her eyes, hear it in her voice, and as she began to jerk into a sitting position, both he and the nurse gently laid a hand on her shoulder. 'Easy there, Charli. Settle back down. Breathe. Deep breaths.'

'Stop telling me what to do.'

'They're just suggestions, but if you settle back and start to breathe normally again, I'll tell you why you're here.'

'Here in hospital?' She sounded sceptical.

'You were found a few hours ago, unconscious down a ravine not far from the Venus Baths.'

'The Venus what?'

'It's a nature walking trail in the Grampians.'

'And before that?'

'Well, today is Tuesday morning and two days ago you were in Melbourne at a medical conference. You were the keynote speaker.' He watched her closely while he spoke. 'You don't remember any of this, do you?'

'Of course I do.' Her words were tinged with impatience. It was the only way she could successfully hide the rising level of panic she felt still rising up within her. She had to remain calm. She had to figure this all out and for the moment she guessed her only option was to believe the man before her.

Maree came in for a moment. 'Wil's here,' she told Logan, and started doing Charli's obs. 'Temperature is 34.7°C.'

'Good.' Logan nodded.

'BP is 120 over 70. Pulse and respiration rates almost normal. Oxygen sats 97 per cent.'

'Good. We'll leave the oxygen on for a little longer, Charli, but you're progressing faster than I'd anticipated so perhaps you hadn't been out on that ravine for as long as I'd previously thought.' A moment later, Wil came into the cubicle. 'Ah, here's our friendly neighbourhood police officer. Charli, this is Wil. Do you feel like talking about things now?'

'N-no.' She stopped, cleared her throat and then closed her eyes. 'I'd rather do it later.'

Logan picked up on her apprehension. 'All right. We'll be taking you off to X-ray soon, so for the moment take the opportunity to rest and you can tell Wil what happened later. Maree's going to take some blood and get the rest of your tests under way.' He lowered his tone and said to Maree, 'The mask can come off before she goes to X-ray if you're happy with her vitals.' Maree nodded and, after giving his patient a concerned glance, he signalled to Wil that they should talk outside.

They left the cubicle and went to get a drink. 'Something's wrong,' he said to his friend after they'd sat down and were drinking their coffee.

'With the coffee?'

'No, with the patient.'

'What? She looks perfectly healthy to me.'

'Something's wrong. She's not recalling details properly. She thought she was in America.'

'America?'

'Yes.' He took a sip of his coffee and thought out loud. 'It's quite common for people who have suffered hypothermia and concussion to be confused.'

'And she's had both.'

'I know but I have a gut feeling there's more to it than that.'

'How do you know her again?'

'She was the keynote speaker at the conference I went to last weekend.'

'Did you…you know…?' Wil grinned excitedly. 'Hit on her?'

Logan laughed, not wanting to tell his mate that Charli had asked him for a drink. 'Yeah, right, mate. I'm hardly in a position to show a woman a good time when I have two children in tow.'

'They're great kids and any woman would be crazy if she passed them up,' Wil defended. 'So she was a speaker, eh?'

'Yes. She's been doing several research projects over the past few years, as well as heading the emergency department at a Los Angeles hospital. She presented some interesting findings on her previous projects, especially one where she's developed this new technique for surgery as well as inventing the piece of equipment you need to do it with.'

Wil held up his hand to stop his friend. 'Spare me the medical details.'

'Let's just say that she impressed everyone at the conference.'

'I can believe it. Smart *and* beautiful. What a combination.' Wil shuddered.

Logan laughed. 'That type of woman scares the life out of you.'

'Absolutely, mate.' Wil sipped his coffee. 'There's one thing that puzzles me.'

'There's more than one that puzzles me,' Logan mumbled.

'How did you know how old she was? Do they usually go around broadcasting the guest speakers' ages at your strange medical conferences?'

'Not usually, but in Charli's case it was a matter of defining who she is. She'd finished medical school by the time she was twenty. She'd specialised in emergency medicine a few years later and has done quite a lot of extra study as well as presenting her research ever since.'

'So she's *really* smart,' Wil stated, and Logan laughed again.

'Way out of your league, mate, and mine too for that matter. Besides, she's an American and has to be back in the States next week to present her results on her latest project. Chances are she'll be discharged from the hospital tomorrow and head back to the States as soon as possible.'

'You sound a little disappointed.'

'Well, it would have been nice to talk to her one on one about some of her research.'

'Is that all?' Wil wiggled his eyebrows up and down suggestively. Logan only laughed. Wil had no idea how close he was to the truth. The instant attraction Logan had felt for Charli was very much there but he still didn't understand what she was doing here...in the Grampians. If she'd been coming to see him, as he'd suggested, why hadn't she tried to contact him? He'd told her what hospital he worked at, that he was a GP in Halls Gap—he wasn't *that* hard to find.

'I'd better get back. Hopefully she's in X-ray now and we can get this show on the road.'

'So she'll be here if I want to talk to her?' The two men stood and headed back the way they'd come.

Logan frowned remembering the way Charli had seemed

frightened at the prospect of staying here overnight. 'I'm not sure. I'd like her to stay but she's adamant about leaving. She'll either be here or back in Halls Gap or wherever she's staying, so you'll get your chance to question her.'

'Let me know if you figure out what might be wrong.'

'It's all just an instinct.'

'Yeah, but in the past your instincts have usually been right.'

Logan nodded. 'I'll keep you informed.' He checked with the nursing staff where Charli had been taken and was told she was in X-ray so he headed there. He couldn't see her or her bed anywhere. For a moment he wondered whether she'd disappeared. She'd certainly been acting strangely enough, and as a doctor would know how hospitals worked. It would be easy for her to escape and hide.

Then he turned his head as a bed was pushed through into a different X-ray room—a bed with Charli Summerfield on it. 'Good.' He crossed to her side. Her eyes were still closed. 'How's everything going? Are the staff treating you well?'

Charli opened her eyes at his voice. 'Dr Hargraves.'

Good. She'd remembered him. 'Call me Logan,' he said with a smile.

'Where am I?' She reached out and grabbed his arm, thankful for the instant comfort she felt in his touch. The look in her eyes was urgent.

'The name of the hospital?'

'Yes.'

'Stawell Hospital.'

'And where exactly is Stawell?'

'About three hours from Melbourne.'

'Melbourne, Australia,' she said, and he nodded. 'You said I'm here because I was at a conference?'

'Yes. I attended the conference. We met—briefly.'

She let go of his arm as abruptly as she'd grabbed it. 'I don't remember.'

Logan nodded, not surprised at her extreme agitation and confusion. 'Let's start with what you *do* remember. Where were you born?' he asked.

'Los Angeles.'

'Where do you live?'

He received a blank stare from her so he thought he'd give her an easy one. He knew she'd overheard him talking when she'd been brought in so he'd test how good her memory was since then.

'How old are you?'

'Thirty-one.'

'What's your name?'

'Charli Summerfield.'

'What is Charli short for?'

She paused before saying with certainty, 'Charlotte.' She sighed and smiled at him. Logan nodded.

'What's your home address?'

Charli opened her mouth and then stopped.

'What happened to you when you went for your walk earlier this morning?'

Again, he received a blank stare from her.

'What was the research you presented at the conference?'

'New techniques in emergency medicine, as well as a prototype for intricate scanning within the bounds of ER medicine.'

'When is your birthday?'

Blank stare.

'How old were you when you graduated from medical school?'

Another blank stare.

'What is your mother's name?'

'Catherine.'

They stared at each other and he watched as despair crept into her gaze. A nurse interrupted them and handed Logan the scans of Charli's spine. He took them out of the packet and held them up to the light so she could see.

'Everything looks fine here. Let's get this cervical collar off your neck. The least I can do for you at the moment is to make you comfortable. And these things,' he said as he took it off, 'are far from comfortable.'

'So what's next?'

'I'd like you to have a CT scan. You're having trouble remembering things, Charli. There has to be a reason for that. Just hitting your head wouldn't be enough to trigger amnesia. The fact that you were out in the cold may have added to things but there has to be another reason. Can you remember being sick lately? Travelling to anywhere other than Australia?'

Again she thought and then shook her head. She glanced down at her hands and then looked at him, her eyes wet with unshed tears, her teeth biting her lower lip. 'If you hadn't met me before today, I wouldn't have even remembered my name,' she whispered.

'I know.' He placed a comforting hand on her shoulder. 'Let's see if we can get to the bottom of this.'

'OK.'

'I'd like to do a few more tests.'

She took a calming breath in and forced her tension away. 'Tests? Like shock therapy?' She raised an eyebrow and it was then Logan realised she was teasing. A slow smile spread across his face. He was impressed. Even when she was facing the unknown, her sense of humour was there.

'I don't think we need to go that far, but if it will make you happy I can organise it. After all, you're going to be here for the next twenty-four hours at least. We don't want you to get bored.'

'I don't think shock therapy will be necessary and neither do I need to stay in for observation.'

'There, I disagree.'

'I don't want to stay here, Dr Hargraves.'

'Logan,' he corrected.

'I know your name, I just chose not to use it. And, anyway, if you don't discharge me, I'll discharge myself.' She lifted her chin a little. It was a defiant gesture and Logan realised there'd be no arguing with her.

'Where are you staying?' he asked pointedly.

'I...I can't remember.'

'Then I think you should stay here.'

'No.' The word was out of her mouth so fast, it surprised her.

'Why not?'

She hesitated. 'I can't remember.' This time she said the three words clearly and with meaning. 'It's just a feeling I have. I don't want to stay here overnight. I hate hospitals.'

Logan choked on a laugh. 'But you're a doctor.'

'That's right. I *work* in hospitals. I don't *stay* in them.'

'They always say doctors make the worst patients.'

'That's me to a T. So will you release me?'

He watched her closely. She really was frightened and she had no idea why. Something wasn't right. Finally, he nodded. 'You can come home with me until we find out where you were staying. I'm *presuming* you were staying in Halls Gap. I'll get Wil to check it out.'

'The cop?'

'Yes. Your memory since you regained consciousness seems fine. You're retaining information as well as recalling snippets of things from your life, such as your mother's name.'

'I don't remember meeting you before. Do we know each other well?'

'No. We were introduced, I shook your hand at the conference and...' He cleared his throat, recalling exactly how he'd felt when he'd touched her. 'And that was about it.'

Charli thought hard but, no, she couldn't remember any of it. 'So I'm in Australia and I came out here to speak at a conference.'

'Yes.'

'OK. At least that's a place to start.' She swung her legs over the side of the bed. 'But I won't be staying with you. I'll check into a hotel.' She paused. 'You do have hotels in Halls Gap, don't you?'

'Yes, but you're better off staying with me. That way, I can monitor you throughout the night and make sure you're all right. I don't have to explain the risks of concussion to you, Dr Summerfield, so you can stop being the high-and-mighty genius that you are and just accept someone's help when they're trying to give it.'

Taking her back to Halls Gap to the surroundings where she'd experienced her trauma might make it easier for her to remember. The more he thought about the idea, the more he liked it.

'Oh, can I now?'

Logan didn't back down from the challenge he saw in her eyes. After all, he had a seven-year-old daughter he had to deal with every day. Charli Summerfield should be a snap!

'Yes, you can. You will either stay with me or stay here in the hospital. Take your pick, Doctor.'

'I'll sign myself out.'

'I'll have you sedated.'

'That's unethical!'

'Not if I think you'd be a danger to yourself.'

Charli leaned back against the pillows and crossed her arms over her chest, her gaze intent on his. 'You wouldn't dare.'

Logan leaned a little closer and she caught the scent of him. It was spicy and earthy and very appealing…and for a brief flash, she knew she'd smelt it before. She shoved the thought aside, determined to stand up to this man and force him to give way.

'Try me,' he said softly, although his voice carried the full weight of his words. In that instant Charli wondered whether she'd met her match. Usually, she'd been able to make any man kowtow to her. It was one of the reasons she'd become head of unit, and she was used to dealing with insolent staff…but not here. Not here in some remote part of Australia where she seemed to be trapped.

'Very well. I'll return to your home with you but I want the police to know where I am at all times.'

'Wise move.'

'Now that that's decided, I suggest we get the rest of my tests done so I can get out of here as soon as possible.'

CHAPTER TWO

LOGAN had to give Charli credit for her behaviour. For a person who confessed to disliking hospitals, she put up with being poked and prodded, eagerly looking at the scans with him and doing everything she was told.

'Your obs are normal and we've found you some clothes. I'll send Maree to help you dress and then we can get going.'

'Sounds good.'

Logan nodded and left her to it before organising her discharge. Next, he went in search of Wil.

'Thanks for sticking around, mate,' Logan said as he walked into the small kitchenette where Wil was rinsing his cup.

'No problem. You ready to leave?'

'Yes. Charli's just getting changed. I'm taking her back to my house for the moment so I can monitor her tonight because she's refusing to stay here.'

'Has she remembered anything more?'

'No, but as I said earlier, between concussion and the hypothermia, she's bound to have some confusion. You can ask her some questions in the car or leave it for later today, but I don't think you're going to get much out of her.'

'What about her tests?'

'Everything's come back normal. CT scan, X-rays—she's fine but there's something definitely bothering her.'

Wil nodded. 'I'll get the car, you get the patient.'

'Actually, can you get the patient, have her sign out and I'll meet you at the car. I just need to get my backpack and a textbook from the hospital library.'

'OK.'

Charli had finished dressing, had two extra blankets around her and was being led out to the clerical area when the policeman came up to her.

'Hi. I'm Wil.'

'I know who you are. I remember meeting you before.'
Charli's tone was brisk and radiated impatience. She watched
his eyes widen in surprise and realised her direct manner was
intimidating him. Good. At least there was one man around
here she'd be able to control. Logan Hargraves was impossible—in more ways than one.

'Uh…OK. So…er… Well, that's good. Logan said you're
staying with him at the moment. That's good.' Wil nodded.
'His kids aren't too noisy but at least they'll be a diversion
for you.'

'I'm sorry. Did you say kids?'

'Sure. Logan has two of them. Kids, that is. A girl and a
boy.'

Charli was puzzled but relaxed a little, feeling some of her
earlier tension disappear. If there were children in his life then
chances were he was married. It made her feel better about
staying with him, but for some reason she couldn't help feeling
a little disappointed that he was already taken. She shrugged.
He was a good-looking man, of course he'd be married.

The topic of their conversation came into view.

'All signed out?'

'She's just doing it now,' Maree said, handing Charli a pen.

Charli scanned the papers quickly before signing her name
without thinking. When she'd done it, she stopped, looked at
the pen and then looked quickly up at him. 'Well, at least that
proves I'm really Charli Summerfield.' She sighed, amazed at
how the knowledge relaxed her.

'I guess it does. Come on, let's get you out of here. Thanks,
Maree.' He turned and said to Wil, 'Charli hates hospitals.'

'But she's a doctor,' Wil said, and Logan chuckled. They
headed out to the car and Logan held the rear door open for
her.

'I'll sit in the back with you.'

'To monitor me?' she asked a little facetiously.

He smiled and she felt her insides twist with pleasure again.
'No. I just thought it was a good opportunity to make a pass
at you.' His plain speaking surprised her and then, when he

laughed, she realised he was teasing her. 'Of course it's to monitor you.'

Wil was laughing, too. 'Logan? Make a pass at someone? Now, that's funny.' Wil started the engine. 'It's been so long, I'm sure he's forgotten how.'

'Keep it clean,' Logan told his friend. 'We don't want to scare our international guest. She probably thinks all Australians are insane.'

'Only those of the male species,' Charli said sweetly, as she took her jewellery from the plastic bag and put it back on. She glanced out the window. 'If I had driven to Halls Gap, would I have come along this road?'

'Probably not. When coming from Melbourne, which we're presuming you were, you would have come via Ararat.'

'I don't remember.' Charli shook her head and Logan thought he detected a hint of fear in her words. Gently, he reached out and took her hand in his, giving it a little squeeze. Heat flooded through her at his touch and again she had a flash that she'd felt this way with him before. It was a nice feeling, a secure one, and she clung to it. She turned to look at him, her eyes wet with unshed tears. 'I don't remember any of this and it's...' She cleared her throat. 'It's scary.'

'I can well imagine,' he said softly.

'No. You don't understand. I can remember the most basic things like how to drive a car or how to insert a catheter. I can remember how to do a laparotomy and I can remember the most minute details of practising medicine—but I can't remember my own name! I only know it because you told me and then signing, just now, confirmed that but...' She broke off and tried again. 'It's...annoying, frustrating and downright scary.' Charli was starting to shake and for the life of her she couldn't stop. 'I've never come across anyone with amnesia before. Have you, Logan?'

'A few times, but it's more of amnesic aphasia in elderly patients. Never someone with the extent you appear to have.'

'Then how am I supposed to fix it? I want to know what I need to do to get my memory back.'

'One thing I can tell you, which I guarantee you won't want

to hear, is that the more you think and dwell on it, the harder it will be to remember.'

'You're right. I don't want to hear it.'

Logan smiled. 'If you stay with me for a few days at least, give your bumps and bruises a chance to heal and let Wil here find out a bit more information about how you came to be in Halls Gap, hopefully your memories will start returning. In the meantime, we can read up on everything we can find about amnesia so we know the best way to handle it.' He pointed to the book he'd just collected from the hospital.

'Information.' She nodded as though this was her lifeline. 'Now, that's something tangible I can bank on.' She took a few deep breaths and then realised she was still holding onto Logan's hand. She let it go and glanced at him, feeling a little embarrassed.

Logan smiled, remembering how she'd held onto him at the conference as well. It was a nice feeling. 'It's OK to show *some* emotion, Charli.'

'Not to a stranger.'

His smile increased and she felt a few cracks appear in the wall which was built around her inner self. 'I hate to break this to you but as you can't remember the past, *everyone* around you is a stranger, whether they know you or not. On that scale, as I'd met you briefly before you forgot your nearest and dearest, I'm almost the best friend you have.'

Charli watched his blue eyes sparkle with sincerity. There was nothing vindictive about him. She realised that without her memories she would need to follow her instincts, and her instincts about Logan Hargraves were that he was a good man. Definitely eye candy too, but that was neither here nor there in the medical world.

What about in her personal world? Her heart asked the question and her head went to brush it away before she stopped and thought some more. She had no idea what kind of relationships she'd had in the past.

Was she married?

Engaged?

Divorced?

None of the above?

'Stop trying to figure it out,' Logan said softly.

Charli looked at him and sadly shrugged her shoulders. 'I can't help it. It's the way my mind works. I have a puzzle and I need to solve it. It's not something I can just switch off.'

'The downside of being a genius?'

'I'm not a genius, I just have a high IQ.'

Logan raised an eyebrow and she realised that in simply saying things in a calm and controlled manner, she'd remembered something about herself. 'At least, I think I do.'

Logan laughed. 'You do. When we get back to my house, which…' he looked out the window '…isn't far now, I'll show you your write-up in the conference programme and the notes I took at your lectures.'

'Thanks. I'd appreciate it.'

Wil brought the car to a stop outside Logan's house. 'I'll check around at the bed and breakfasts and other accommodation places to see if you were registered anywhere. Depending on what I find, we'll see where we go from there,' Wil said as his two passengers climbed from the police car.

Logan nodded. 'Ring me, regardless of the information.'

'Will do.' With that, Wil drove off, leaving them standing outside Logan's single-storey brick home.

'Hold those blankets tight and I'll get you inside. We still need to keep you nice and warm.'

'Where are you going?'

'I need to lock my medical bag in the surgery,' he said, sliding one arm through the strap of the backpack. 'It won't take long. You can come if you'd prefer.'

Charli nodded and followed him inside, noting the security code as he punched it into a panel on the wall. She knew instinctively that she'd remember those numbers for ever and frowned a little. Did she often go around memorising numbers? She thought for a moment and then recited a number off the top of her head.

'What's that?' Logan asked.

'The code for my hospital locker.'

He turned on the light and raised his eyebrows. 'Any other numbers come to mind?'

'Um…18, 12, 68, 37, 88, 73.'

'And that is?'

'My apartment alarm code.'

'Excellent. Once we find where you live, you'll at least be able to get inside.' He continued up the corridor and into the room at the end. 'Come on through,' he called when he realised she hadn't followed him.

'I'll wait here,' she called. He started unpacking the bag and once that was done he went in search of Charli. She was sitting in his waiting room, the blankets around her, flicking through a glossy magazine.

'Anything jump out at you?'

'No, but at least I'm up to date on all the movie world gossip.'

'Ah…probably not as up to date as you think. That magazine's been there for the last two years.'

'What?' She flicked it over and checked the date on the cover. 'You can't shell out for some new ones?'

'Hey. There are new ones there.' He pointed to the tables of neatly arranged magazines. 'But my mother likes to keep the ones that have interesting stories.'

'Your mother?'

'She's a retired nurse and does my receptionist work for me. That particular two-year-old glossy has a very interesting article about self-examination of breasts. Apparently, she's been asked to photocopy the article several times so, as far as my mother is concerned, the magazine stays.' He checked his watch.

'You don't have a clinic today?'

'Yes, morning clinic, which as my watch says it is now after one o'clock, means it's well and truly over.'

'Well, where are your patients?'

'Mum would have cancelled the clinic this morning. It's no big deal.' He shrugged and leaned against the door frame.

'Doesn't that bother the people around here?'

'Quite the contrary. It may put the odd tourist out, but as

for the locals? No. They fought long and hard to get a doctor stationed in Halls Gap so medical help would be available sooner for emergency and retrieval purposes.'

'And as you came out early this morning to…' Charli cleared her throat '…retrieve me, they don't mind waiting until tomorrow to see you for a repeat prescription.'

'Exactly, and if anyone had an emergency, they'd simply go to Stawell Hospital as they used to before I came to this area.'

'And this afternoon?'

'House calls. I was thinking of getting a bite to eat for lunch and then heading out. Want to come along for the ride?'

It was on the tip of her tongue to refuse but she looked around her and realised she had nothing else to do. It was a strange sensation.

'Come on,' Logan urged when she didn't answer right away. 'We'll make sure you're rugged up. I can't imagine someone like you likes being idle, but on the other hand, if you have a headache or feel like a rest after this morning's ordeal, it's no problem if you'd prefer to hibernate in your room. Alternately, you could just watch some television.' He stood up straight. 'Come through to the house, I'll fix us lunch, show you the stuff from the conference and then you can decide.'

Charli stood and nodded. She'd expected him to go out the front door but instead he headed to the rear of the building and stopped in the corridor next to a door. He took out his keys and unlocked it. 'This connects my house to the surgery. Makes it easy when I'm running late.' He set the surgery alarm again and they went through the door into an external walkway. She waited again while Logan unlocked another door into his house.

'Good to see that you're tight about security. Usually small townsfolk don't bother locking their doors.'

'We have a lot of tourists around and personally, as there are drugs kept on the clinic premises, I prefer to keep everything under lock and key.' He walked through the door into his house and then turned to hold it open for Charli. 'I guess it's one of those things which has stayed with me from when I lived in Melbourne.'

'How long ago?' she asked as they walked down the hall-way into the kitchen.

'Since I lived in Melbourne? Just over five years.'

'Any particular reason why you left?'

Logan shrugged. 'Necessity.' He began taking things out of the refrigerator. 'Salad sandwiches for lunch?'

'Sounds great.' Charli sat down at the kitchen table and looked around the room. There were pictures up on the walls of Logan and his family. There were drawings and paintings stuck on pin-boards as well as notices and birthday cards. She could hardly see the surface of the fridge or freezer due to the magnets which covered them. It all seemed foreign to her—but then she remembered that *everything* was foreign to her.

'Try not to think about it.' Logan said the words softly and she realised he'd been watching her. There was compassion in his tone and Charli appreciated his concern. She also felt a frisson of awareness at the way he was looking at her so in-tently. 'We'll get to the bottom of things. You'll see.' He smiled then and she wished he hadn't. Compassion, concern and then one of those heart-melting smiles was enough to knock any woman off balance. Charli forced herself to look away and gave herself a stern lecture in self-control. She had to remember that Logan was a married man. He was not avail-able.

'Now, would you like a cup of tea or coffee? Or some soup? What can I get for you?'

'A domesticated male. How refreshing.'

Logan laughed. 'Out of necessity.'

'Tea would be nice, thank you.'

'Coming right up.' Logan continued to work in the kitchen while Charli looked around the room. There were bookshelves behind her and she swivelled in her chair to study them.

'I see you're quite fond of the classic fairy tales.'

Logan smiled as he carried the food to the table. 'Yes, and I'm not kidding when I tell you I've read each book on those shelves at least twenty times over, if not more. We have four different versions of the *Three Little Pigs* and I can probably recite each one word for word.'

'Quite an accomplishment, Doctor. Is that on your résumé?'

'No, but I think it should be.' Before he sat down, he disappeared from the room and returned a moment later with a leather folder. 'This is the information from the conference,' he said, and laid it in front of her.

Charli looked at him, her eyes wide with fear, but it was quickly veiled as she took a deep breath before opening the folder. There were the usual pieces of paper about the conference and its aims. A list of people who would be presenting papers. She noticed Logan's name on the list. 'You presented a paper?'

'Yes. Emergency medicine in small towns.'

'A favourite hobby of yours?'

'No. More…necessity.'

Charli looked at him critically. 'Necessity to present the paper or necessity to do the emergency medicine in a small town?'

'Both, actually.'

'And do you do everything in life by necessity, Logan?' Her tone was almost critical but he realised it was just a smoke screen. Still, the question was a valid one.

He smiled politely. 'Sometimes.' He knew she was stalling and she knew he knew. 'Would you like me to read out the section about you?'

Charli's gaze dropped back to the papers in front of her. 'No. No. I'll read it myself.'

'OK.' Logan sat in silence, watching her as she flicked through the pages until she came face to face with a picture of herself. Even though her hair was pulled severely back into a chignon and her lips were only slightly curved into a tight smile, the eyes, the nose and the high cheekbones were all the same.

They were all *her*!

Charli read the biography about herself, desperately trying to feel the things she read. She'd certainly accomplished a lot in her life. She was thirty-one years old and had completed medical school at the age of twenty. She currently held the position Director of ER at a Los Angeles hospital. She continued to read the brief of her talks and then scanned the notes Logan had made from her lectures.

When she'd finished, she looked at Logan. He'd finished his drink and his sandwich while she hadn't even touched hers. Still, he was watching her closely.

'Trying to figure out what I might be thinking?'

Logan merely smiled.

'Well, I'll tell you. I'm thinking how can I read this about myself and it feels like I'm reading about someone I don't know? Shouldn't I *feel* something? Have at least some sort of mental reaction? Instead…nothing.'

He nodded. 'It may *feel* like nothing but it's definitely a place to start. We know where you work, which means they'll have a listing of where you live. You've already remembered the security code to your apartment, and once you're back in your own environment the chances of your memory returning are quite high.'

'I thought you didn't know that much about amnesia.'

'I don't, but from what I remember, what I've just said is the usual prescribed course of action.'

'That and not thinking about it?'

'Right.'

'Oh, you're a valuable fount of information, Dr Hargraves.'

Although her words were dripping with irony, Logan merely smiled and accepted them. 'Why, thank you, Dr Summerfield.' He motioned to her sandwich. 'Are you going to eat that?'

Charli eyed the sandwich and then shook her head. 'Not hungry. Sorry.'

'Hey, don't apologise.' Logan dragged the plate in front of him. 'Saves me making another one.' He picked up her lunch and began to eat. Charli watched him in surprise. 'What?' he said, after swallowing a mouthful. 'You hadn't touched it. I wasn't about to let it go to waste and I was still hungry.' He took another bite, chewed and swallowed. 'I guess in Los Angeles you just toss food away left, right and centre.'

Charli levelled him with a glare. 'I wouldn't know,' she said pointedly.

'*Touché.*' Logan laughed, his blue eyes twinkling. Charli felt her hackles rise at his attitude and he watched her closely. 'You have that same look in your eyes that my daughter gets when I've said something wrong.'

'Sounds as though she's an intelligent young woman.'

'She is.' Logan finished off the sandwich before standing and carrying the dishes to the bench. 'You've got to mellow out a bit more, Charli. Sure, you can't remember and, believe me, I didn't mean to be rude, but try not to take everything to heart.'

'Perhaps that's just the way I am.'

'Perhaps. Perhaps now is your opportunity to find out who you really are deep down inside.'

'Meaning?'

'Meaning all you have to follow at the moment are your instincts.'

The fact that his words mirrored her earlier thoughts surprised her.

'We're each born into a certain way of life and we go along with that life, sometimes questioning, sometimes following—'

'Sometimes doing what's *necessary*?'

'Exactly.' He stacked the dishwasher and turned it on. 'You, on the other hand, now have the opportunity to simply follow your instincts. Listen to your heart instead of your head. Find out who you really are.'

'Do you know something about me? Something you're not telling me?'

Logan crossed to her side. The woman he'd met in Melbourne had been uptight, brisk, efficient and looked as though she hadn't laughed—*really* laughed—in a very long time. How was he supposed to tell her that? It was only his own gut instinct and observations which had told him that. Maybe he'd been wrong in those assumptions. 'No. I told you. We were introduced, we shook hands and that was it, Charli.'

'Honest?'

'You were stressed, overworked. More so than your average genius.'

'I don't like that label being applied to me, Logan.'

'Understood. Actually, I'm not surprised your brain has shut down in this way. It was either that or you were heading for a mental breakdown.'

'And you know this how?'

'Observation. Instinct. Look at your write-up in the conference folder and tell me when in the last fifteen years of your life you haven't been studying or working or researching something. Probably *longer* than fifteen years. When would you have had time just to relax? To play? To do something special for yourself?'

Tears began to prick behind her eyes. His words, somehow, made sense…and she didn't like it. 'How am I supposed to answer that?'

'You're not. I'm just saying I'm not surprised your mind is refusing to remember. It's on holiday. Gone fishing.'

'Gone fishing?'

'It's an expression. Why don't you try and enjoy your self-inflicted break?'

'You don't think there could be anything else? Anything that might have caused my brain to…to go fishing?'

Logan thought back to her skittish behaviour as she'd all but tugged him into the lecture hall. Now he wished he'd looked over his shoulder to see who she'd looked at which had triggered her reaction. Hindsight.

'I can't answer that.'

'Can't or won't?'

'Both.'

'You're protecting me.'

'I'm giving your brain a chance to rest a little. You have to relax, Charli, or you'll just find yourself going around in circles like a dog chasing its tail.'

'But I don't know who I am!' The words were whispered with total fear and the tears which had been threatening to fall before slid silently down her cheeks. Logan groaned, wanting nothing more than to gather her close to him and never let her go. Instead, he handed her a tissue.

Charli wiped her eyes and blew her nose before putting the tissue in the bin. Then she reached beneath the collar of her top and pulled out the chain. 'This says, "Love, Chuck" on the back.' She watched as Logan stared at the love-heart pendant, his jaw clenching slightly. 'Who's Chuck? Do you have any idea?'

'No.'

'Was I with someone at the conference?'

'You had a personal assistant but I think his name was Ira. I'll let Wil know and he can check it out with the conference committee. Perhaps this man Chuck was registered.'

'I just need to know,' she said, her voice still wobbly. 'It's only been a few hours and already it's driving me crazy.'

'I know. As hard as it is, let's leave the detective work up to Wil. He'll be contacting the hospital where you work to get some information. We'll get to the bottom of this. I promise.'

Charli took another tissue and blew her nose again, feeling a little better. 'I know.' She bit her lower lip to stop it from trembling. 'But that's all? That's all you remember from the conference?'

Logan raked a hand through his hair, appearing a little self-conscious.

'What? Tell me, Logan.'

'We…well, we shared a…moment.'

'You and I?' His words didn't surprise her. There was something…she had no idea what but there was definitely something between them. 'A moment? What's that supposed to mean?'

'You asked me out for a drink.'

That jolted her. 'What about…Chuck?'

'Hey, you asked me.' Logan paused. He didn't like it one bit that she was wearing a necklace which might indicate she was already spoken for. Then again, she *had* asked him for that drink. How he wished, now, that he'd taken her up on her offer. 'Perhaps Chuck is your brother or a family friend or something.' At least, that's what he was hoping.

'Did you come? Did we have a drink together?'

'I couldn't.' Regret was clearly in his tone. 'I had to work.' The way he was looking at her, the way his gaze held hers in such an encompassing way, made her feel as though she were the only person in the world he cared for. There was no pity, no judgement. It made her feel…special. It made her feel…nice. The word seemed so insignificant but nevertheless it was a nice feeling which warmed her through and through when Logan Hargraves looked at her like that.

It was then she realised she was also powerless to look away. Their gazes remained locked and time seemed to stand still. In those moments she saw a veiled passion burning deeply in his blue depths and the knowledge stirred her all the way to the centre of her being.

Her eyes widened in surprise and Logan knew he had to break the contact between them—the words which weren't being spoken by either of them—but it was extremely hard to do when the urge to move closer to her and capture her lips beneath his kept growing stronger and stronger with each passing second.

Charli shifted in her chair and the sound of the wood scraping against the wooden floor jarred them both. Logan took a step backwards and raked a hand through his hair again. 'I'd better get ready for house calls,' he mumbled, before stalking from the room.

Charli sighed and slumped forward on the table. What on earth had just happened? Was that the same as the 'moment' he'd just referred to? Logan was a married man and a married man had no business looking at another woman the way he'd just been looking at her—just as she had no right to be looking at him in exactly the same way. She might not remember anything about her past, but of those facts she was certain. And then there was the mysterious Chuck. *Was* he her brother? She thought hard but no answers appeared.

She sat up, gathered all the papers together and placed them back in the leather folder. She knew Logan was getting ready for house calls and she had to decide whether to go with him or whether to stay here, in this foreign house…alone with her thoughts.

'Coming or staying?'

She jumped as he spoke from behind her.

'Sorry. I didn't mean to startle you.'

Charli stood and turned to face him. 'That's all right. I was lost in my…thoughts.' As she said the words, she smiled. '*Very* lost.'

Logan returned her smile, glad she was making a joke herself. 'Coming out for house calls or would you rather stay here and rest?'

'I'll come with you, if that's all right.'

'Not a problem. Let's get you rugged up, then.'

He gave her one of his pure-wool jumpers and one of his jackets to put on.

'Gorgeous,' he said, when she glanced down at herself.

'I hardly look like the picture-perfect professional from your conference information.'

Logan shrugged and picked up the black medical bag he'd packed earlier. 'Let's go.' He headed towards the front door, holding it open for her and then locking it behind her. 'There are only three patients on today's list so we should be home just after noise time.'

'Noise time?' They walked out to a blue Jaguar and Logan once more held the door for her. 'Thank you,' she responded, trying not to breathe in too deeply as his scent seemed to surround her.

'Noise time is the time between half past three and half past seven, Monday to Friday.' He grinned at her as he walked around to the driver's side and climbed in. They had their seat belts on and Logan started the engine before he said any more. 'Those are the hours between my children coming home from school and going to bed. Four hours of constant noise.'

'Sounds as though you're not looking forward to it,' she said as he reversed out of the drive and turned onto the main road.

Logan smiled. 'And miss the squabbling, the excited chatter, the tired laughter and all those hugs and kisses? Never.'

'You enjoy being a father?'

'You sound surprised.' Logan glanced across at her, wondering how much experience she'd had with children. There was no point in asking, he realised as his mind began formulating questions to ask her.

'I guess I don't know much about it—parenting, that is.'

'I don't think anyone does. Unfortunately, there's no manual and you just have to muddle through the best you can, using your common sense.'

'That's it?'

'Well, that's all I've been doing.' He laughed as he turned into a street and then into a driveway. 'Mrs Jenkinson,' he said as he set the handbrake and cut the engine, 'suffers from emphysema. She's not been doing too well lately. Spring isn't a good season for her so instead of her coming to see me in the clinic, I drop in and check on her once a week, sometimes twice a week, depending on her needs.'

'Isn't that the sort of thing a community nurse would do?'

'She does. Between the two of us we share the job of checking up on those patients who need a little more attention.' Logan climbed from the car and Charli followed him. 'Besides, the district nurse who works this area also works most of the Grampians so her schedule is sometimes busier than mine. I don't mind doing these house calls and it gives me the opportunity to keep in touch with everyone on a regular basis.' He collected his bag from the car and then headed to the front door. He knocked twice before twisting the handle and going inside.

Charli wasn't far behind him but she could still smell his scent and it was starting to drive her insane. It was so fresh and spicy and warm and yummy… And then she realised it was the clothes she was wearing which were doing the damage. She shook her head, determined to block the information coming from her smell receptors.

'Mrs Jenkinson?' he called, and headed into the kitchen where he found her sitting at the table enjoying a cup of tea.

'Oh, Logan, dear,' the elderly woman wheezed. 'Come on through. Oh, look, you've brought a friend.'

Logan introduced Charli as a colleague who was visiting from overseas and left it at that. 'Have a seat, dear. Cup of tea?' Mrs Jenkinson coughed her way through her words but didn't seem to mind. She had an oxygen bottle beside her and a tube around her ears which ran beneath her nose.

'Thank you.'

'And what about for your new friend?'

'Er…no, thanks, Mrs Jenkinson.'

'Ooh.' Mrs Jenkinson stopped and coughed. 'You're American. How lovely. If I'd known you were coming I'd have baked some scones.'

Charli looked at Logan, trying to figure out why Mrs Jenkinson would have baked scones, but Logan merely shrugged, indicating he didn't know either. Charli smiled and decided to wing it.

'I'll pour, shall I?' Logan asked, and Mrs Jenkinson seemed happy with that. He continued to help out by offering Charli one of the cookies from the plate on the table. She took one and thanked her *real* host.

'How have you been during the past few days?' Logan asked once everyone had a drink and some food. He knew his patient wasn't satisfied until everyone who came to visit had had something to eat and drink.

'Not bad, dearie. This poor old woman is getting worn out.'

'Well, I have some good news for you. The blood test you had last week when you came to the clinic has come back quite good. Your arterial blood gas level is closer to normal, which, as this is spring, isn't bad.'

'Oh, that is good news, dearie. Isn't that good news?' she asked Charli, who nodded.

'Has the physio been helping much?'

'Oh, yes, but you know, I'm trying to stay indoors as much as possible so I don't breathe in too much wattle.'

'Wattle?' Charli was interested.

'It's a flower, dearie. Bright yellow, beautiful to look at but not good for those of us who have trouble breathing.'

Logan drained his small teacup and rubbed his hands together. 'Let's get your check-up under way, then.' He listened to her chest and did her obs while Charli chatted politely.

'Lost your memory!' Mrs Jenkinson gasped in horror, then proceeded to have a coughing fit. 'Oh, dear. How dreadful. Just as well Logan's looking after you, then. He's such a brilliant doctor. We all love him, don't we, dearie?'

'I have many fans,' he remarked with a satisfied smile.

'His kiddies would be the biggest fans. He's done wonders for those children.'

'I've hardly done it alone.'

'You expect it of grandparents. It's just the way the world is now. Oh, and would you mind asking your mum to do another copy of that breast self-examination article in that magazine for my great-niece, please, dearie? I'd be ever so grateful.'

Logan's smile was smug as he looked at Charli. She rolled her eyes, acknowledging his smugness, but didn't say anything.

'She'd be delighted to do that for you, Mrs Jenkinson. Now, if we could just check your peak flow, that should about wrap everything up for today.'

'All right. I'm feeling a little tired after the day's exertions.'

'I know exactly what you mean.' They did the test and Logan noted the results before packing his equipment away. 'Prescriptions are fine? Don't need any more?'

'No. I'm fine, dearie. If you'd just help me to have my medication and get me into bed, I'd be grateful.'

Logan and Charli did just that and let themselves out of Mrs Jenkinson's house.

'She will be all right, won't she?' Charli climbed into the passenger seat, feeling strange there wasn't a steering-wheel in front of her, and turned to face Logan.

'Her daughter will be home within the next twenty minutes to take care of her.'

'Good. Where to next?'

'Angie Morrisey. She's forty-nine and works at the general store in town—and I do mean *general*. That place sells everything, including the most delicious ice creams you've ever tasted. You'll have to try some while you're here.'

'I'll put it on my list. So what's wrong with Angie Morrisey?'

'She hasn't been feeling too good lately. She came to the hospital on Sunday evening…' Logan stopped and glanced across at Charli. If he hadn't driven back to Stawell and worked that night, they would have had a date after the conference. Even if they'd *had* the date, Charli wouldn't remember it. He pushed the thought aside.

'Sunday evening…' She prompted.

'She felt lethargic, had a sore throat and a cough. There was nothing wrong, though. Chest sounded all right, throat was a touch red but nothing out of the ordinary. I gave her a complete check-up but everything seemed fine. I told her I'd check on her this afternoon just to touch bases and make sure everything's OK.'

'Maybe her symptoms were emotional? Has she had any big upsets recently?'

He looked at her again and smiled. 'Don't tell me you're a holistic doctor as well?'

'Our emotions drive our everyday living so why wouldn't they affect our health? Stress, for example, is triggered by emotions as well as situations.'

'You know, you could be right where Angie is concerned. Her daughter is doing her last year of high school and will be going to university next year.'

'First one to leave the nest?'

'Yes.' Logan pulled up outside Angie's house and they walked to the door together. He rang the bell and waited. 'How are you feeling? Are you warm enough?' He placed the back of his hand on her forehead and Charli jerked back, her eyes wide with surprise from his touch. 'Sorry. I didn't mean to startle you.'

'I feel fine.' Or at least she had before he'd touched her. Now she felt as though a fire had spread through her, reaching all the way down to the tips of her toes. How could he affect her so easily? Concentrate, she told herself sternly.

Logan rang the bell again and frowned. He tried the handle but it was locked. 'Angie?' he called, and banged on the door. No response. 'I don't like this. Stay here in case she comes. I'm going to try the back door.' He raced off, leaving her with his medical bag.

Charli waited where she was. A few anxious minutes passed where she kept ringing the bell and banging on the door, calling out to Angie. Then she heard Logan calling for her and grabbed the bag before rushing around the side of the house.

'Logan?'

'Over here.' He'd opened the back door and disappeared back into the house. Charli followed quickly and it was then she realised he was on the phone, giving the address. He rang off as he walked back through to the kitchen. 'Angie? Angie? Can you hear me?'

Charli crouched down beside the woman. 'Pulse is weak. Skin is cool and clammy.' She opened the medical bag and pulled out his torch. 'Pupils equal and reacting to light.'

'There's an oxygen cylinder in my car,' he told Charli. 'Stay here with her while I get it.' He raced out and was soon back, fitting the non-rebreather mask over Angie's nose and mouth before turning it on. 'Just breathe, Angie. Breathe.'

Charli had the stethoscope on and was listening to Angie's chest. 'Very tight.'

'Angie? It's Logan.'

Angie murmured and moaned.

'Where's the pain?' he asked. 'What's happening, Angie?'

'Chest, arm, neck,' she panted. 'Logan? I'm scared.'

'I know you are. Do you know how long you've been on the floor?' As he spoke, both he and Charli worked to try and diagnose what was wrong.

'I don't know. I didn't feel well and I was heading to the phone and—'

'Shh. It's all right now. We're here.'

'BP's decreased. Is there a history of angina pectoris or heart attacks in the family?' Charli asked the question and Logan shook his head.

'Not that I know of.'

'My uncle,' Angie said breathlessly.

Charli had loosened Angie's clothing and was listening to her chest again. 'It's tight. Try a nitroglycerine tablet under her tongue and we'll see if that does any good.'

Logan nodded and retrieved a tablet from his bag. 'I'm just going to lift the mask and I need you to keep this under your tongue,' he told Angie. 'If it's going to work, we'll know almost immediately.'

'Hope so,' Angie panted.

Thankfully, it did and Angie reported the constrictive sensation lifting. 'It was like someone was standing on my chest and I just couldn't breathe.'

'Close your eyes and relax,' Logan soothed. 'You'll be fine. The ambulance is on its way.'

'Ambulance?'

'It's all right. Just relax, I said.'

'But I have to go to work.'

'I'm sure Mrs Blackwell will understand,' Logan said with a chuckle. 'You need to go to hospital, Angie, and that's all there is to it. Where was Philip working today?'

'Out past Horsham.'

'I'll get Wil to get a message to him.'

'BP's better, pulse is better, chest sounds as though she's getting a lot more air into those lungs of hers,' Charli reported.

'Good.' Logan looked at his colleague. 'I could get used to this.'

'What?'

'Not having to do everything myself.'

Charli smiled at him and continued with the observations. Angie looked up at her.

'Who are you?' she asked, and Logan begged her forgiveness and introduced the two women. They waited for the ambulance to arrive and once Angie was settled in and Bruce and his partner had whisked her away, Logan packed up his bag, locked Angie's house and walked back to the Jag.

'Whew!' He exhaled a long breath and turned to smile at Charli. 'I'm glad you were here, Doc.'

'You would have coped fine without me.'

'I'm saying thank you, Charli. Just say "You're welcome, Logan", and then we can move on.'

'Why are you saying thank you?'

'I believe in giving credit where credit is due,' he said with a curious frown. Hadn't this woman ever been praised for doing a good job before? He thought back to her high IQ and wondered whether great things had just been *expected* from her so people had forgotten to thank her. He shook his head and checked his watch. 'Noise time has begun. We'd better get back.'

'What about your other house call? I thought you said you had three?'

'I do. *You* are my third but I can check your vital signs back at my home.'

'I'm not your patient, Logan.'

'I beg to differ.' He walked to the car, holding the door for her. When it looked as though she wanted to stand there, her chin raised in a defiant gesture he was coming to recognise, he shrugged his shoulders and headed around to the driver's side. He'd climbed in, put his seat belt on and started the engine before she moved, quickly getting into the car.

'Some doctor you are,' she growled as she pulled on her seat belt. 'Leaving your patient standing in the middle of nowhere, especially when she doesn't know who she is.'

'But you do know. You're Charli Summerfield. We know your name, we know where you work and those are all places to start. Now all we need to do is figure out how you got to Halls Gap, where your clothes, belongings and, more importantly, your passport are and then we can get you on the next plane home. Once I've cleared you fit to fly,' he added.

'Lest we forget, you're my bossy doctor.'

Logan chuckled. 'Yes, I am, and thank you for admitting it.' He pulled into his driveway and climbed out, collecting his bag. 'I'll just dump this in the clinic before—'

His words were cut off as the door to the house across the road banged open and two children started running straight for him. Both stopped at the kerb and quickly checked there were no cars coming before heading over, their arms flung out, wide, happy grins on their faces.

'Too late,' Logan muttered, and placed the bag on the ground. He knelt down on one knee and opened his arms wide, ready for the onslaught.

'Dad!' the girl yelled, and the boy was in hot pursuit of his sister. Both had deep brown eyes and Charli realised they must have inherited the gene from their mother as Logan's eyes were a definite blue.

'Daddy!' The children hurtled themselves into his arms and knocked him backwards to the ground. Logan had an arm around each of them, rolling around and obviously tickling them as the peals of laughter rang out with shouts of 'Stop it, Dad' and 'I'll tickle you, Daddy'.

Charli simply stood there and watched, amazed at the sight before her. It was foreign. She couldn't remember anyone ever holding her like that. A picture of her mother's face flashed into her mind and she gasped. The expression on her mother's face was one of pride. Maternal pride. She was proud of her daughter, of her accomplishments, and her mother loved having a daughter who was smart. That was all Charli could remember but that one little snippet was enough to make her tremble.

Logan glanced over to see Charli watching them. Her eyes were wide and as she raised a hand to her mouth he realised she was shaking. 'Hold on, hold on.' The kids grabbed onto him and he levered himself up into a standing position. 'All right. Inside, and you can have two cookies each.'

'Yay!' He held out the house keys to Trinity and both of them ran off, delighted at the treat waiting for them inside. Logan crossed to Charli's side.

'You've remembered something,' he stated.

'Yes.' Charli turned to smile at him, an unsure, watery smile. 'Nothing big, nothing dramatic. I just remembered that my mother was proud of me.'

'That's a nice memory.'

Logan was smiling at her again. Smiling the way he'd been earlier on. The moment of happiness she'd experienced vanished as the new sensations of awareness once again began to swamp her. His wife. His wife. She had to think about his wife.

'Uh… What time…' she took a step away from the car '…does your wife get home?'

'My wife?' He looked at her as though she'd grown an extra head.

'Yes. The woman you're married to? The mother of your children?'

'Oh! *That* wife.' He shook his head. 'I don't have one.'

'You don't have one?'

'No.' He smiled at her.

He wasn't married?

'Did she die?'

'No. I've never been married.'

He wasn't married! He wasn't *married*!

Something didn't add up. 'But…your children?'

'They're my brother's children. He and his wife died in a car accident not long after Owen was born.'

'So you just stepped in and took over?'

'Sure.' Logan shrugged and collected his bag from the ground.

'Necessity?'

'You could say that.'

'So you're *not* married.' She just wanted to get things straight.

'No.' When she didn't say anything else, he said, 'Any other questions?'

'So you're the legal guardian of your brother's children?'

'Yes.'

'And the house across the street?'

'My parents'.'

'Ah, the mother, retired nurse and clinic receptionist who doesn't throw out the old magazines.'

'Got it in one. Gee, you really *are* a smart lady, Charli.'

His blue eyes were twinkling and she realised immediately he was teasing her. 'Oh…go soak your head.'

He laughed. 'I'd better get inside before they eat *all* the cookies. Want to come?' He held his hand out to her in an innocent gesture of friendship. A split second passed as a multitude of thoughts raced through Charli's mind.

She wanted to accept his gesture, to hold hands with him, to be free enough to do so and to go inside and snag some of those cookies for herself. She needed to relax, enjoy herself— after all, that was her doctor's prescription!

But another part held back. It wasn't the proper thing to do. She hardly knew this man and the thought of touching him, holding hands with him, set her instantly on fire. His touch had affected her before and she knew it would now.

But so what? He *wasn't* married and... She glanced down at her fingers. Although she wasn't wearing any rings, she checked for a tan line which might indicate a more permanent commitment but there was nothing. As for Chuck, well, she had no idea who he was and—

'It's only cookies, Charli.'

Logan interrupted her thoughts, his blue eyes still teasing her.

'You're right.' Taking a deep breath, Charli put her hand in his and, smiling up at him, they went into the house together.

CHAPTER THREE

THE Hargraves household was a madhouse! After two hours with Logan and the children, Charli had a headache. She'd watched in fascination as Logan had fielded questions, supervised homework, signed notices for school, cooked dinner and patiently explained why people have belly buttons when Owen had asked the question over a mouthful of mashed potato.

'I'm exhausted,' she muttered as he came into the kitchen after tucking his children into bed. 'How on earth do you do this day after day after day?'

Logan shrugged and checked the coffee pot. 'You just get used to it. Is this fresh?'

'Yes. I needed a strong cup.'

He laughed as he poured himself some coffee and pulled a stool around so they were sitting on opposite sides of the kitchen bench. 'They're...boisterous.'

'Thank goodness they're asleep.'

'Oh, they're not. Trin will be out in about ten minutes with a concern. "Daddy, I couldn't sleep because I'm too hot, or too cold." "Daddy, I had a nightmare."'

'And what do you do then?'

He shrugged. 'Deal with it.'

'You don't think she should stay in her room until she falls asleep?'

'You sound like my mother. I don't know whether there's a wrong or right thing to do but if something's bothering her, I'd rather she talks about it.'

'How did you learn all this?'

'What? Parenting? You don't.' He took a sip of his coffee. 'You just deal with each situation as it arises.'

'They're just so...full on.'

He smiled. 'Especially Owen, but I didn't get them like this. I've grown with them. To begin with, it was hard. Trin was

57

always looking for her mother and Owen, well, he was used to being breast-fed and suddenly he had a bottle shoved in his mouth, which, I might add, he didn't appreciate one little bit.'

'So while you were grieving for the loss of your brother and sister-in-law, you also had to deal with two children.'

'I didn't do it alone, Charli. My parents have been there every step of the way. We sat down, discussed what was best for the children and those two little ones became our first priority.'

'They know you're not their father? They call you Dad.'

'I'm all they can remember. They both have pictures of their parents in their rooms. We've made no secrets of the fact that they're not my biological children.'

'And they just accept that?'

'Kids are resilient, Charli. It's a pity sometimes adults can't be the same.' He drained his cup. 'I need to unpack my medical bag and get started on some paperwork.'

'What's your plan for tomorrow?'

'I'll do a catch-up clinic in the morning and then I'm rostered on at Stawell Hospital tomorrow afternoon and evening.'

'And the children?'

'Go to their grandparents whenever I'm working. Mum or Dad will come here and put them to bed if I'm not home, and stay with them until I do get home.'

'You seem to have all the bases covered.'

'It's a system we've devised so the children have the best.' She was looking at him in stunned amazement. 'What?'

'You're a very generous man, Logan Hargraves.'

'I wouldn't say that. I just do—'

'I know, I know. You do what's necessary, but you wouldn't be able to do that without such a giving and caring heart. I may not have a clue who I am, but I know that what you're doing is rare.'

He felt embarrassed at her words. 'Thank you for your words but I'm not doing it alone and I get back more from the children than I put in. I love them.'

The words were said with the utmost simplicity and Charli marvelled at it. They both stared at each other, neither one game enough to break contact first but both wanting to do so. The phone rang and Logan walked out of the room to get it.

'Dr Hargraves.'

'Logan, it's Wil. How's the patient?'

Logan heard the teasing in his friend's voice and smiled. 'Physically, she's fine.'

'You can say that again.'

'Get your mind out of the gutter.'

'And mentally?'

'Not so good.'

'Meaning?'

'Charli has amnesia.'

'Amnesia? Wow. What happens next?'

'It means the puzzle of her being in Halls Gap is harder to unravel than we thought.'

'How bad is her amnesia?'

'She has retrograde amnesia, which means she can't remember anything before we found her.'

'What's the treatment?'

'She has to relax.'

'That's it? I thought you said she was a bit forgetful due to the hypothermia and concussion.'

'That's what I initially thought and, sure, those factors have increased her symptoms, but the reason she can't remember is because something emotional has happened to trigger repression of certain memories. The medical term is hysterical amnesia.'

'I'll need to speak to her.' Wil was in policeman mode.

'I'll put her on so you can have a word with her,' he said as he walked back towards the kitchen, taking the cordless phone with him. He stopped just outside the room, watching as Charli stood there, her eyes closed. She was so beautiful. He didn't want to interrupt her but he knew she needed to talk to Wil, to tell him about some of the things they'd discovered so far. He cleared his throat, knowing her eyes would instantly snap open.

She turned to face him and he held out the phone. 'It's Wil.'

Charli nodded and accepted the receiver, trying her best not to look at Logan. The look they'd shared before the phone had given them a timely interruption was still smouldering deep down inside her. How could this man she'd known for less than a day make her feel so overwhelmed with emotion? But right now he was the *only* person she really knew so perhaps that was why the attraction between them felt strong. He was a giving, caring, compassionate man and at the moment she needed that type of person in her life.

'Hello, Wil.'

'Charli…er Dr Summerfield, er, Dr Charli.'

'Charli's fine, Wil.'

'Er…good. Uh, I've checked and come up empty on accommodation in Halls Gap. You weren't booked in anywhere but there's one thing I *have* found. Do you remember driving here?'

'No.'

'Do you remember hiring a gold sedan?'

'No. Why?'

'A gold car has been parked in the car park outside the general store all day. The keys were in the ignition but no one has returned to claim it.'

'This is odd?'

'It may not be in a big city but here, yes, it's odd.'

'What's next?'

'I'll ring the car rental place in the morning and see if I can get a lead on whether or not it was you who hired the car.'

'Sounds good.'

'I've also contacted the hospital where you work and they have you down as being on leave until Thursday next week. Apparently, you have a big international meeting next Wednesday evening so I'll be contacting the American Consulate to find out what we need to do about getting you a new passport.'

'OK.' So that was why no one had raised the alarm. She'd been missing for almost a whole day and as far as she knew, or as far as Wil was telling her, no one had missed her because she wasn't due to be missed. 'Thanks for that information.' Charli closed her eyes, feeling dejected, miserable and alone.

'What about my mother? Was the hospital able to give you a contact number for my mother?'

'Yes. I was just coming to that. I've called and left a message on her answering machine. I'm just hoping she'll get back to me.'

'Good.' Charli told him about the few things she'd remembered and he agreed to make it his top priority. 'Thanks, Wil. I really appreciate your help.'

'Well…uh…it's my job.'

There was silence on the line for a moment and Charli felt another round of apprehension wash over her. 'Was there anything else?'

'Er…yes.' He cleared his throat. 'Er…how are things going at Logan's?'

She sighed as she realised he was asking as a concerned friend, rather than from a police point of view. It was a nice gesture so she didn't bandy words when she answered. 'Good. He's quite bossy and his kids are really noisy, but apart from that…' She trailed off when Wil began to laugh.

'OK. I'll leave you to it, then, and I'll keep you informed.'

'Thanks. I'd appreciate it.' She handed the phone back to Logan who spoke to his friend for a few more minutes, walking out of the room so Charli couldn't hear what they were saying. When he returned, he found her putting their cups into the dishwasher.

'I've just thought of something else.'

'What's that?'

'You don't have any clothes or a toothbrush or hair things.'

'No. The thought had crossed my mind earlier and…money is an issue, too.'

Logan nodded. 'I think I can solve some of your immediate problems at least.'

He stepped back and appraised her, making her feel immediately self-conscious.

'You're about the same size as my sister-in-law. Come with me.'

She followed him down the hallway, watching in surprise as he stopped to check on both children. 'Owen's out to the world and Trinity's pretending,' he whispered, before continuing down to the spare room. He opened a cupboard door to reveal a rack of women's clothes. 'These were Alison's. You're welcome to borrow them while you're here.'

'You didn't want to get rid of them when she died?'

'Look around this room.' There were boxes stacked neatly in the corner with labels on which said 'Shoes', 'Clothes', 'Misc.'. 'These are all things for the kids so if they want to know more about their parents, they can. Trevor's trophies for athletics, Alison's hairdryer and curling wand. They shouldn't be denied their roots.'

Charli was amazed. She glanced around the room and then back to Logan. 'You're a nice man, Logan Hargraves.'

Her tone was so soft, so genuine that Logan was surprised to find her words tapping at the door to his heart. He gruffly cleared his throat and broke eye contact immediately. 'I just do what needs to be done.' He walked over to where the ceiling vent was and opened it. 'That will let some heat through. The room should warm up soon. I'll get some sheets for the bed and some towels because you'll probably be wanting a shower.' Logan headed for the door. 'I'll see if I can find an extra toothbrush. I'm sure I bought some new ones a few weeks ago but Trin put the shopping away and I'm not quite sure where they ended up.' He grinned, his gaze meeting Charli's once more, and he felt an instant wave of discomfort settle over him. Did she have to look at him like that?

She was all dreamy and misty-eyed and her blonde hair fell slightly across her face, which made his fingers itch to tuck it behind her ear. It was as though she could see right through him, right through the walls he'd built around his heart over the years, and with one little look he could feel those walls starting to crumble.

He cleared his throat again and looked away. 'Be right back.' He had to stop himself from sprinting down the hallway, wanting to escape as quickly as he could. What was it about her that made him feel this way? He liked her. He thought she was attractive yet for some reason he didn't want

Charli Summerfield looking on him as some sort of knight in shining armour when he just wasn't.

He did what needed to be done—and that was all.

Nothing heroic. Nothing superheroish. Just…reliable.

Logan pulled the items he needed from the linen cupboard and returned to the spare room. 'Here you are.' He put the things on the end of the bed. 'I'll go find that toothbrush,' he said, and raced from the room again.

In the kitchen he braced his hands on the bench and forced himself to take some deep breaths. 'Toothbrush. Think toothbrush,' he muttered to himself.

'Daddy?' Trinity's soft, unsure voice made him jump sky high. 'Daddy?' This time her query was one of puzzlement as she looked at him in surprise.

'Sorry, sweetheart. I was in another world.' He beckoned her forward. 'What's wrong?'

'I can't sleep.'

'Hmm. Why not?'

'Because my tummy's sore.'

'Have you been to the toilet?'

'Yes.'

Logan picked her up and carried her to the bench stool and sat, gently smoothing the hair out of her face. 'What's been happening at school?'

'Nothing.'

'Is that a good thing or a bad thing?'

'What?'

'That nothing is happening at school? I would have thought you might be doing some work, playing with your friends.'

'Dad!' She gave him a soft pat. 'I don't mean that.'

'Everything's all right at school?'

'Yes.'

'Then at home? Has Owen been annoying you?'

'He *always* annoys me.'

'He's a boy.'

'Will he grow out of it?'

Logan smiled. 'Probably not.'

'Who's the lady who's here? Is she your girlfriend?'

As far as Logan was concerned, the question had come to-tally from left field and for a moment he simply sat there, stunned. 'Er…no, princess. I hardly know her.'

'Then she's a stranger. You said we weren't supposed to talk to strangers.'

'She's my patient, Trin.'

'She talks funny.'

'She's from a different country.'

'She's pretty.'

'Yes, she is.'

'So you like her, then?'

Logan laughed. 'I told you. I hardly know her, and for that matter she hardly knows herself. Charli has amnesia. It means she can't remember who she is or where she lives or what happened yesterday.'

Trinity nodded solemnly. 'That's hard. It's just like me when I can't remember my mum and dad.'

'In a way, but you've got me and Grandma and Grandad to tell you all about your mum and dad so you know how much they both loved you.'

'And Charli doesn't have anyone to help her?'

'That's why she's here.'

'So we can help her?'

'Yes.'

Trinity yawned and he hoped that what had been bothering her was now dealt with and she could settle down to sleep. 'I'll help, too, Dad.'

'That would be nice and I know one way you can start. Do you remember where you put the toothbrushes I bought the other week?'

'The new ones?'

Logan smiled and nodded.

'I put them in the cupboard in the bathroom.'

'Of course you did. Thank you, sweetheart. Now, off to bed.'

'Tuck me in?' Trinity yawned again and Logan stood and carried her back to her room. He placed her on her bed and pulled the covers up before kissing her on the cheek.

'Sweet dreams, princess. Love you.'

'Love you, too, Dad.' Her eyes had closed and she reached out for her favourite toy to cuddle. Logan smiled down at her before turning and heading out of the room. He went straight to the bathroom and opened the door, only to be met by a yelp from Charli who was standing in the middle of the bathroom floor in her underwear.

'I'm sorry,' he mumbled as she grabbed the towel off the rack and held it in front of her. With his hand still on the doorknob, he turned and headed out again, closing it firmly behind him. 'Sorry,' he said again and stood stock still, unable to move as the mental image of Charli Summerfield practically naked replayed over and over in his mind in a recurring pattern.

He closed his eyes, his grip tightening on the doorknob as he fought to control it. Push it from your mind and check on the kids, was the command that came back. Dragging in a breath, he forced his legs to move and his hand to finally let go. He walked away, checked on the children and then walked directly outside into the brisk evening air.

The coldness hit him with force but it was exactly what he needed. Logan raked a hand through his hair several times as he stood outside. What was a man to do? Her body was…perfection, her underwear was colourful and sexy and the way her hair fell across her pink cheeks was… was…heaven.

The shocked and embarrassed expression he'd briefly witnessed in her eyes completed the picture and he cursed his mind for being able to pick out every little detail after one brief second of looking at her. He felt awful for invading her privacy but it had been an honest mistake. She could just have easily walked in on him.

That thought sent him into overdrive and, although he had his own *en suite*, he decided one of the things to add to his shopping list tomorrow was to buy locks for the bathroom and toilet doors.

Dragging in a few more breaths, he felt calm enough to enter the house once more. He went to the kitchen and poured himself a cup of coffee. He added milk and sugar and sipped it, feeling the warmth flow through him.

When he'd suggested she come home with him, he'd expected Wil to have notified him of a bed and breakfast or hotel room where Charli had been registered. Instead…nothing. Nothing but a car, which they didn't even know for sure had been hired out to her.

Now Charli was not only clueless as to who she was or how she came to be here, she was also homeless. Medically, it was good that she was here for the night. He could monitor her, but he had to admit she seemed perfectly fine to him…in more ways than one.

He shook his head, clearing it of the thought. She was his patient and a guest in his home. She was in trouble, she needed help and he would give it. It should only take a few days to sort things out and then she would be winging her way back to the States and out of his life for ever. A few days. He could do this. He *had* to. The risk of becoming strongly attracted to a woman who lived on the other side of the world was not one he wanted to take. He had responsibilities here—responsibilities he was more than happy to shoulder—and Charli definitely didn't fit into those plans.

Sure, she was gorgeous. He wouldn't deny that. And, yes, it had been a long time since he'd been out on a date or even socialised with a woman so, of course, his hormones would zoom into overdrive. But he was a grown man and one who had learned to control those hormones years ago.

He took another sip of his coffee, feeling more relaxed, more in control and more like himself than he had ten minutes ago.

'Hi.'

Logan looked up to see Charli in the doorway, her hair falling softly around her face, her teeth nipping at her lower lip and her body covered from wrist to neck to ankle in flannelette pyjamas. He swallowed slowly, his control vanishing into thin air.

She looked soft and cosy and cuddly. His hands gripped his coffee mug tighter as she crossed to his side. 'I'm beat.'

Logan's mouth seemed to be full of cotton wool and he swallowed again, trying to get his vocal cords to work. 'I'll, um…' He stopped, cleared his throat and tried once more. 'I'll get that toothbrush for you. Trin said they're in the bathroom cupboard.'

'Oh. I found it. Thank you. I was looking for some soap,' she added by way of explanation.

'Good.' The silence surrounded them and Logan forced himself to think normally. 'Uh…do you have a headache? Need some paracetamol or something else? How's your body temperature? Are you warm enough?'

'I'm quite warm, thank you. Actually, two paracetamol would be great.'

Logan immediately opened a high cupboard door and took out a first-aid kit. 'Here you are,' he said, and put a packet of tablets on the edge of the bench. There was no way he could risk handing them to her in case they accidentally touched. He was far too aware of this woman and he wanted it to stop.

'Is that all you need?' She moved into the room and took the tablets off the bench. 'Wait here and I'll get the sphygmo so I can check your blood pressure.'

'No, Logan.' Charli shook her head quickly. 'It's fine. Really. Apart from being tired with a slight headache, I'm surprised at how good I feel.'

'You sure?'

'Yes.'

'OK, but I will be checking on you during the night.' *She's your patient. She's your patient.* He kept repeating the words to himself, hoping they would sink in.

Charli knew this was procedure. She knew, as a doctor, that he needed to check on her, but the thought of Logan coming into her room in the middle of the night to see if she was all right didn't do much for her equilibrium.

She nodded and then shrugged. 'Well…good night, then, and…and…er…thank you.' She crossed to his side and, rising up on tiptoe, she placed one hand on his shoulder, urging him down a little before she placed a light, feathery kiss on his cheek. 'See you in the morning.'

With that, she turned and left.

One instant she was there, and the next she was gone.

Logan couldn't move. How on earth was he supposed to sleep *now*?

After a restless night, where he prowled the confines of his bedroom, checked on Charli and the children three times and managed a whole hour of sleep…at least he thought he'd slept…Logan was having a hard time keeping his eyes open and his temper in check as he rushed his kids through their morning routine.

So far there had been no sign of Charli and when he'd checked on her at five o'clock, she'd been sound asleep, curled up into a small little ball beneath the blankets, breathing peacefully. Logan sat down at the table, coffee cup in hand, once he'd walked the kids down the road to school. His clinic started in fifteen minutes, which gave him fifteen extra minutes to doze.

He closed his eyes and tried to concentrate on easing the tension in his trapezius. It was where he put all his stress and he could really use a good massage right about now. He wasn't used to the sleeplessness any more. When he'd been training, yes, but now, after five years of being a rural GP where some days he had no patients booked in his clinic and other times when he was flat-strap, he wasn't used to having sleepless nights. The last one he could remember had been when Owen had cut his last tooth.

This time, though, his sleep deprivation was caused by one person—Charli. Logan certainly hoped Wil had some positive news today because he wasn't sure how much longer he could carry on with Charli sleeping under the same roof. Naturally, he would exercise control. She was in turmoil, she was upset and confused, and the last thing she needed was a romantic entanglement, which would only compound the matter even further.

The sound of a spoon dropping made Logan raise his head, and he looked around to find Charli at the kitchen bench. She was dressed in a pair of denim jeans and a pale pink cotton shirt, the shoes she'd worn yesterday on her feet. Her hair was pulled back into a ponytail and she looked about eighteen years old. He felt his gut tighten once more.

'Sorry. I was trying not to disturb you.'

'Uh…it's OK.' He glanced at the clock. 'I need to get to clinic anyway.' He stood and took his cup to the sink. He tipped the remains down the drain and put the cup in the dishwasher. 'How are you feeling?' he asked as he walked towards the door.

'Really good. I had a great sleep and feel refreshed.'

'Glad to hear it.' He hesitated a moment before saying, 'Remember anything in your dreams?'

Charli sighed. 'No.' She frowned at him and then looked away.

'What is it?'

'Nothing.'

'Charli, just say what you need to say. Something's wrong, so come on—out with it.'

'Out with it?' She looked at him in amazement. 'Who do you think I am, Logan? A seven-year-old girl?'

He closed his eyes, realising his attitude wasn't helping. 'Sorry. You're right.' He raked a hand through his hair and took a deep breath, exhaling slowly. He opened his eyes and looked at her. The pink in her shirt made her blue eyes seem more vibrant, if that was at all possible. Focus! 'What is it that's bothering you?'

'How do you know something's bothering me?'

'You seem a little…jittery.'

'I feel a little jittery. I can't explain it but I just don't want to be left alone.'

He nodded. 'That's understandable. You can't remember who you are so you need company or else you'll be left alone with your blank thoughts.'

'Exactly.' She looked down into her coffee cup, hesitating to meet his gaze. Finally she did, and as Logan smiled at her she felt her courage return. 'I was wondering if I could come over and sit in the clinic with your mother?'

'Uh…sure. I don't perceive a problem there.' She saw a

spark of humour in his gaze as he said, 'You can discuss the merits of updating the waiting-room magazines.'

'Yes.' Charli didn't know why but she felt instantly better. She didn't have to be alone.

'It's not just the fact that you can't remember, is it.' His words were a statement and Charli didn't bother pretending she didn't know what he was talking about.

'No.'

'You were nervous and jittery at the hospital, not wanting to stay overnight. Something's not right.'

'You're right…but I have no idea what it is. At the moment I just need to follow my instincts, and they're telling me not to be left alone. It might be because you found me alone in a ravine. I have no memory of being there. Perhaps someone was with me. Perhaps I was pushed. I don't know.'

Logan shook his head. 'Wil had a pretty good look around the area and he couldn't see any signs of a struggle, but he isn't one hundred per cent sure.' He paused. 'It's OK, Charli. We'll get to the bottom of it.'

'That's just the thing, Logan. I don't know if I want to. What if I start to remember and find my life isn't worth remembering? Maybe I've blanked it out for a reason.'

He watched as she became more and more agitated as the words flowed from her mouth. She started to pace around the kitchen, as though walking around helped her put her thoughts into words.

'What if I wasn't happy, but was just going along with my life because that's what you do? You say that I'm a smart person. I don't feel smart right now. I read those papers from your conference and it doesn't seem as though I'm reading about myself. I remember numbers at the drop of a hat but have no idea what they stand for. I'm supposed to be doing research for a multinational company and I can't remember the first thing about it. What if I don't get my memory back? What if, after quite a while, I never find out how I ended up in the middle of nowhere in Australia?

'Then there's my hospital. They said I'm scheduled to be away for another week. What's this international conference

I'm supposed to be speaking at next week? How am I going to do it if I'm stuck in Australia and can't remember what I'm meant to be talking about? My mother isn't answering her phone and that isn't right. I don't know why it isn't right but it just isn't.'

She looked at him and shook her head, her gaze wide with fear. 'I'm scared, Logan. I'm scared to remember and I'm scared not to remember.'

Logan crossed to her side and put his hands on her shoulders. His voice was imploring yet gentle. 'Not thinking about it is the best way for your brain to slowly unlock the door. You're not alone, Charli. Know that for a fact. I'll be here to help you. So will Wil. We're the good guys and the good guys *always* win.'

Charli couldn't help but smile at him, momentarily enjoying the feelings of security, safety and not being totally alone in the world. His hands were warm and instantly reassuring and she knew what this man said was the truth. He *would* stand by her. He *would* help her, and it was a very nice feeling to know she had an ally.

The moment she smiled, Logan instantly dropped his hands from her shoulders and took two huge steps backwards. 'Right, now, how about you finish your coffee while I finish getting ready for clinic?' He glanced at the clock again. 'My mother's going to be yelling for me soon enough.'

'Yelling? Really?'

Logan smiled. 'You'd better believe it. I'll be back in a second.' He headed to his room and forced himself to relax. He didn't much like the thought of Charli spending the morning with his mother for the simple reason that his mother would take Charli under her wing and protect her. Not that there was anything wrong with that, but it would draw Charli much closer into the bosom of his family and at the moment he needed distance from her…as much distance as he could get.

He grabbed a tie from the drawer and put it on, before heading back towards the kitchen. 'Ready?' he asked. Charli looked across at him, smiled and nodded. The small action caused his gut to tighten and he immediately pushed the sensation away. She quickly stacked the dishes in the dishwasher.

'Do you want me to put this on?'

'I'll do it later.'

'It won't take a moment, Logan, and it's full.'

He knew his smile was strained. All he wanted was to get out of the intimate atmosphere which would continue to build if he walked into the kitchen where he would be able to smell the subtle scent of whatever it was she was wearing. He couldn't remember seeing any perfume with his sister-in-law's things but, whatever she'd found, it was definitely working on him…and he didn't want it to.

Still, she was right. It would take a few seconds to put the dishwasher on and then he wouldn't have to worry about it later. He quickly crossed to the kitchen, making sure he gave her a wide berth, working automatically as he put the powder into the machine and set it going.

'Sorry, Logan. I didn't mean to push. It's just that it—'

'It's fine.' He wiped his hands on the towel and walked towards the door.

'Logan?' Charli was thoroughly confused by his attitude. He seemed to be running hot then cold, and it wasn't at all like the man she'd met yesterday. Yesterday? Was it only yesterday they'd met? It seemed like a lifetime. Well, to her it *was* a lifetime—as much as she could remember of her life at any rate.

He stopped, turned and impatiently raked a hand through his hair. He'd hurt her or at least confused her by his briskness, and it wasn't what he'd intended to do. The woman was gorgeous! Didn't she realise that? Didn't she realise she could make his blood boil just by the way she was looking at him? He wanted to look away but he couldn't. There was definitely something between them. Something neither of them should pursue and definitely something neither of them had asked for. It was just…*there*.

Charli sucked in a breath as she looked into his eyes as he turned. It was then she saw it.

The desire smouldering beneath the surface and his behaviour started to make perfect sense. Charli couldn't help a similar feeling from stirring within her and then bursting to life. Knowing deep down that what she was about to do was ridiculous as well as stupid, Charli slowly crossed the room to stand in front of him. His gaze held hers the entire way, both mesmerised by the other.

Logan could feel the tension mounting inside him with every step she took. Closer and closer she came while the burning within him turned into a raging furnace and he prayed it was one he'd be able to control.

'Logan?' This time there was no confusion in her eyes, in her body language, in her question. What Logan saw this time was a woman who was in complete control of her faculties, and he wondered if she knew that when she looked at a man with a passionate fire in her gaze, it was enough to burn the man up completely. That was how she was looking at him now and Logan knew, without a doubt, that if he didn't kiss her immediately, he would regret it for the rest of his life.

'Charli.'

Her name was a caress on his lips and she loved the way it sounded. For one moment she honestly felt that Logan cared for her, that she was the sole focus of his life. Even though the logical side of her said otherwise, she pushed it away and concentrated on the here and now…and now she desperately wanted Logan's lips on hers.

He moved closer, her heart pounding fiercely against her ribs. As their bodies touched, her chest against his, Charli was astounded at the explosions that coursed through her.

With barely any movement, his arm came around her waist, drawing her even closer. Lowering his head to hers, he brushed his lips briefly across hers and then pulled back a little to check that this was what she really wanted.

He saw what he wanted to see in her eyes.

The acknowledgement that she needed this as much as he did.

CHAPTER FOUR

'Logan!'

The sound of his mother's voice was like a bucket of icy cold water thrown over the two of them.

Logan dropped his arm from Charli as though burnt, and quickly stalked up the corridor to where his mother had entered his home through the external walkway.

'Mum.'

'There you are. You have two patients waiting to see you and as you have to go to the hospital this afternoon, I don't want you to run late. Besides, it isn't fair that people have to wait because the doctor needs to finish his cup of coffee.'

'I've finished my coffee,' Logan muttered. He turned to look back the way he'd come and saw Charli standing hesitantly not too far away. 'Mum, let me introduce you to Charli Summerfield. Charli, this is my mother, Rose.'

'Pleased to meet you, Mrs Hargraves.' Charli stepped up next to Logan and extended her hand. As she did so, her arm accidentally brushed Logan's and she gave a mild gasp, immediately covering it over with a smile. She ignored the tingles that flooded through her at the mild touch and instead forced her concentration on the handshake she was receiving, as well as what Logan's mother was saying.

'Call me Rose, dear. The town's too small to stand on ceremony. First names all round. Now...' Rose dropped Charli's hand and gave her a concerned look. 'How are you feeling, dear? Headaches? Nausea? Anything like that?'

Charli was touched at the other woman's concern. 'No, thank you. I'm fine.'

'Charli was just asking if she could come and stay in the waiting room with you this morning while I do clinic.'

'Of course, dear. The people in town are already a little curious about you so it will be nice for them to meet you.'

74

'They know about me?'

Rose laughed. 'Of course, dear. Wil's been asking around the town to see if anyone had seen you or knows anything about how or why you came here. You're a great mystery and we're all looking forward to helping you unravel what's gone on.'

Logan glanced at Charli, wondering how she felt at being described as a 'great mystery'. As soon as he'd done it, he realised he should have just walked past the two women and started his clinic. At that moment she'd glanced up at him and their gazes held for a nanosecond before Logan found the strength to look away...but that brief moment had been enough to register the smouldering desire still evident in both of them.

'I'll get started,' he muttered, and headed next door. 'Get a grip,' he lectured himself. Now was not the time to think about what had almost happened. The feel of his lips on hers in that one brief, feather-light touch only let him know what he was missing. In that frozen part of time he'd experienced a red-hot desire he'd never felt before. He shook his head, calling on his professional training to pigeonhole the incident so he could concentrate on his clinic. He walked out to the waiting room, apologised to his patients and called the first person through.

As the morning progressed, he found himself reluctant to go out to the waiting room to call his patients through. Charli was sitting out there, obviously having a good time chatting to people and having lively discussions with his mother. She was smiling, laughing, her eyes twinkling and bright. It was killing him!

Just after eleven o'clock, the phone on his desk rang. Logan excused himself from his patient and picked up the phone, expecting it to be the pathologist from Stawell with some news on Angie Morrisey's results.

'Logan.' His mother's voice came quietly down the line.

'Yes.'

'Harriet Ardnaught has just called through to say that Amelia's pulled a cup of tea off the table and it's landed all

over her neck, shoulder and chest. Harriet's beside herself, but
I told her to keep Amelia under running cold water while she
gets things ready, not to take her clothes off and to wrap her
in a cold, wet towel and bring her in immediately.'

'Put her straight into the second examination room and no-
tify me as soon as she arrives. Ask Charli if she wouldn't mind
getting things ready in there. She's probably more experienced
with these things than I am.'

'I'll get it organised.' His mother rang off.

'Everything all right?' Arnold Blackwell, the patient who
was with him, asked, and Logan told him what had happened.
'I'll tell my missus to make sure young Harriet's other kids
are picked up from school and looked after.' Arnold stood up.
'Hope the poor little one's all right.'

Logan agreed and finished writing out Arnold's prescription. 'Thanks, mate. Come and see me next week if that hasn't
cleared up by then.'

'Will do.'

Once Arnold had left, Logan wrote up his file and headed
to the second examination room he kept set up for emergencies
just like this. Charli was opening cupboards, checking out his
stocks, pulling a few things out and putting them on the treatment trolley.

'Where are your IV lines, Logan?'

'End cupboard. What's the best way to handle this?' Logan
checked what she'd put out on the trolley and went to the sink
to scrub. Once he was clean, he put on a white gown and then
grabbed a new cotton sheet to drape over the examination
couch before placing sterile drapes on top.

'Wet the drapes for a start. We need to keep her cool. Your
mother said the child is two—is that correct?'

'Yes.'

'Up to date with immunisations?'

'Yes.'

'Good. We'll need to get oxygen into her as well as IV
lines, stat. Do you have a child-size mask for the oxygen?'

'Yes.' Logan went to a cupboard and pulled one out.

'We need to maintain her airway, assess how deep the burns

are and then treat accordingly. Most scalding incidents are first- or second-degree burns and children find it harder to cope than adults.'

'There's no point in transferring her to Stawell, then.' Logan nodded. 'I'll get Mum to organise a retrieval team from the children's hospital in Melbourne.'

'They'll send a helicopter?'

'Yes. It lands on the sports oval.'

'Is that close?'

'No. We'll need Bruce here with the ambulance to transfer her there.'

'OK. If you can do her obs, IV line and analgesics, I'll monitor the burn wound.'

'Right.'

'She's just pulled up,' Rose said as she stuck her head in the door. Logan gave his mother the instructions for Amelia's ongoing care once they had her stabilised. Charli and Logan both pulled on a set of gloves and a moment later a sobbing Harriet carried little Amelia through.

The sound was deafening as the toddler let everyone in town know that she was hurt.

'Nothing wrong with her lungs and vocal cords by the sound of it,' Logan whispered to Charli. He made sure Harriet wasn't left out of the loop and explained what they'd be doing. They gently unwrapped Amelia from the towel and looked at the wound site.

The right side of her neck, shoulder and chest, from what they could see around her clothing, were already turning a mottled white, pinkish colour.

'She needs to know you're still here. She needs her mum. Talk to her, soothe her.' His voice was calming, hoping it would have the desired effect on both mother and daughter as he worked beside Charli, performing the neurological observations.

Harriet was mopping at her tears but did as she was told.

'It's OK, sweetheart,' Logan said as he looked down at Amelia. He was ready to put the IV line in but the little girl was so upset he was hard pressed to keep her arm straight. As he held her arm, she glared up at him, her brown eyes red and puffy from crying as she tried once more to push the oxygen mask off her face with her left hand. 'We're going to get you sorted out, aren't we, Charli?'

'Yes, we are,' Charli responded as she began cutting away her clothes.

'Harriet, I need you to hold Amelia's arm for me. It needs to be still so I can get the IV line in.'

'Why does she need it?'

'We need to keep her fluids up as at the moment her body is sending all fluids to the areas which need them most. Also, once the line is in, I can give her something for the pain.'

Harriet tried to hold her daughter's arm but it wasn't working. 'I can't,' she cried.

Logan smiled at her. 'It's all right. Can you ask my mother to come here, please?'

Harriet left Amelia's side for a moment and the child began to cry harder. 'She's coming back. She is,' Logan promised. Harriet was back in her position like a shot and Rose came up behind her son.

'I need you to hold her arm for me so I can get the IV in.'

'Right.' Rose firmly held the child's left arm and then leaned over, blocking Logan from the child's view. She soothed some hair away from Amelia's face and kissed her forehead. 'Hello, princess. It's going to be all right. Don't you worry about anything. No.'

Amelia's cries began to decrease. 'That's a good girl,' Rose continued to soothe, long after Logan had the IV line in place. 'OK. What a brave girl you are.'

'You're a whizz with kids, Mum.' Logan smiled at his mother, thankful the noise in the room had decreased. 'Poor baby.' He looked down at Amelia, who was now whimpering and snuffling. 'How are you doing, Harriet?'

'OK.' Harriet stepped closer when Rose moved away.

'If you need me again, let me know,' Rose said.

'Thanks, Mum.' Even though he'd been preoccupied with the IV line, Logan had been watching what Charli was doing.

Carefully, she'd cut the clothing not stuck to the skin away to reveal the extent of the burns.

'She has splash patches on her right thigh and knee. She already has blisters and the skin just under this piece of clothing...' Charli lifted the corner with a pair of tweezers '...is almost cherry-red. Mild to moderate oedema.'

Amelia started to cry again and Logan drew up some midazolam. 'This will help her with the pain,' he told Harriet and administered it through the IV. 'Won't be long, sweetheart. You're being a very good girl.' He looked at Charli. 'Diagnosis?'

'Second degree, at least.'

Logan nodded and began performing the obs again. 'Slow improvement,' he said after listing his findings. When the ambulance and chopper finally arrived, Logan was glad little Amelia was stabilised.

'She'll be fine for transfer to Melbourne,' he told Harriet.

'What about the other kids?' the mother gasped. 'I'd totally forgotten about them.'

'Don't worry,' Rose said, coming up behind Harriet and giving her a hug. 'Mrs Blackwell's already organised everything. One of your neighbours will meet you at the sports oval with an overnight bag for you and also Amelia's favourite toy.'

'And Kurt? What about him?' Harriet asked Rose as they walked behind the stretcher to the ambulance. Logan and Charli climbed in beside Amelia and made room for Harriet.

'We'll get a message to him. You go and be with Amelia. She needs you.'

Harriet sniffed and nodded. Logan met his mother's gaze and mouthed, 'Thank you.' Rose closed the ambulance doors and soon Bruce was driving them to the sports oval. Harriet held her daughter's hand, trying hard to be brave. Charli checked the burns area once more, diligently caring for the small child. Logan watched her, amazed at how great she'd been. Of course, he'd expected nothing less from the head of an emergency department but, still, it was so good to have someone else there to help carry the weight.

Logan checked the drip and changed the bag over. 'You're doing a good job, Harriet,' he said softly.

'I can't believe I wasn't watching her. She shouldn't have been in the kitchen and I'd just made a cup of tea and it was on the bench and I didn't know she could reach that high. Why wasn't I watching?'

Logan nodded, knowing exactly how she felt. 'I know it's easy for me to say and hard for you to do, but don't beat yourself up, Harriet. We can't watch them twenty-four seven, and sometimes these things happen. Remember when Owen was two and he fell out of the window?'

Harriet looked at him and nodded. 'Yes.'

Logan shook his head. 'I *still* feel horrible about it. How could I have let that happen? Why hadn't I been watching him? Why had I left the window open? I knew he was a climber. He climbed on anything he could—still does, for that matter.' He smiled and placed a hand on the other woman's shoulder. 'But he was all right. A mild bump on the head but Owen was fine and he still *is* fine. Kids are resilient, they bounce. It's us adults who store the memories and emotions. Amelia's only two, and by the time she's six she probably won't remember much of this. You, however, will have it for ever in your catalogue of memories. That's a fact. Another fact is, the more you mentally beat yourself up about it, the harder it's going to be for you to get Amelia through this. That's what you have to focus on now. Be strong for her, be happy when she sees you. She'll cope so long as you cope. There's nothing you can do to change what's happened so try really hard to let it go.'

'I know what you're saying…but it *is* hard.'

'Of course it is. That's part of the parenting thing.'

Harriet gave him a watery smile. 'Thanks, Logan. Alison would be proud of the way you've raised her kids.'

'Thank you. That's nice to hear.' They were pulling up at the sports oval, and when the rear doors opened Harriet stepped out first. 'How's her skin looking?' he asked Charli as he performed the obs again and wrote down his findings.

'Still not good but it's over to the plastic surgeons now.'

'I'm glad she's stabilised for the journey.'

'Me, too.'

Amelia was taken over to the helicopter and loaded on while Logan and Charli gave their report to the retrieval team. Harriet climbed on board, her overnight bag stowed at her feet, her focus entirely on her daughter.

They all stepped back as the chopper started, and once it was gone, Harriet's neighbour spoke to Logan for a few minutes before leaving.

'I'll give you a ride back,' Bruce said, and they all clambered into the ambulance. He dropped them back at Logan's house. They went inside and found Rose clearing up.

'No more patients?'

'No. The hospital called through with Angie's results.' Rose handed them over. 'I've cleaned the second examination room and just need you to finish up on a bit of paperwork from today's activities and then you're free to go.'

'Thanks.' Logan accepted the files. 'Oh, I forgot to mention that Mrs Jenkinson wants a copy of—'

'The breast-examination article?' Rose finished. 'Yes, I know. Charli told me.'

Logan looked at the woman in question. 'Thanks. OK, so I can have lunch now?'

'Yes. I've arranged with Mrs Blackwell for me to have Harriet's kids for tonight. That way I can pick all four children up from school, feed them and get them ready for bed. It's also a treat for Josie and Mikey, which they'll need as both of their parents will be in Melbourne with Amelia.'

'Have you managed to get hold of Kurt?'

'Yes. I called through to Planet Electronics and he's going to drive straight to Melbourne. I suggested he stop by home and get a change of clothes for a few days which, once he calmed down, he said he'd do.'

'He's driving by himself?' Logan was concerned. 'Kurt's not good with pressure and stress, especially where it concerns his family,' he explained to Charli.

'I agree, so I spoke to Jon and he said Marty was at the

plant and was heading back to Melbourne so would take Kurt with him.'

'Excellent. All right. I'll get these done during lunch and then I'm off to the hospital.' He glanced at Charli. 'Ready to eat?'

She shrugged. 'I guess so.' They headed to Logan's house, leaving his mother to finish up at the clinic.

'Now, if I make you lunch today, will you eat it?' He set the notes down and headed for the refrigerator.

'Yes.' She sat on the stool at the bench. 'Planet Electronics.'

'What about them?'

'They're *here*? In the Grampians?'

Logan realised she was remembering things but didn't want to break her chain of thought. 'The plant where Kurt works is in Heartfield, which is south-west of here. It's not in the Grampians themselves but a lot of people who live here work there.'

'Planet Electronics?' Charli asked incredulously.

'Yes.'

'The people who are branching into biomedical technology all around the world?'

'Yes. Why? Did you want to meet the guys responsible?'

'You *know* them?'

'Jon and Marty. Sure. Their sister, Halley, is a doctor in Heartfield.'

'I've been looking for a company to make the prototype for a new piece of computer software I've designed. It's all a bit rough but I've been very impressed with what I've read about Planet Electronics.'

Logan nodded, a slow smile crossing his face. 'And what's that?'

'Well, they're reliable for a start. They always deliver, their overhead costs aren't too exorbitant and they have the staff and equipment I need. I had no idea they were so close to where I am now.'

'Amazing.' Logan leaned on the bench, just watching her, waiting for her to realise she was remembering. When she gasped in wonderment, he couldn't help laughing. 'You're cute.'

'Don't tease me.'

'I'm not.' He started making sandwiches for lunch but couldn't keep the smile from his face. 'You just start talking and I don't want to interrupt in case I block the memory.'

'So this is how it's going to be. Little patches at a time.'

'I guess so.'

'How far away is Heartfield?'

'It's about half an hour from the lower end of the Grampians, down Dunkeld way. And before you ask…' he held up his hand to silence the question he could see forming 'Dunkeld is about an hour's drive south from Halls Gap.'

'And Planet Electronics have the plant there.'

'Yes. It's almost out in the middle of nowhere.'

'And you know the doctor there.'

'Doctors—plural. Halley married Max Pearson and they both run the hospital there. They have three children and their oldest is the same age as Trinity, so it makes it easy when we want to get together for a barbecue or something social like that.'

'So they help you out in big emergencies and vice versa?'

'If it's a big search and rescue, yes.'

'I can't believe I'm so close.' She paused. 'I can't believe I remembered everything just like that!' She snapped her fingers and laughed. 'It's such a nice feeling.'

Logan enjoyed her mood while they ate lunch. He quickly wrote up the case notes for his mother and then, without even needing to ask, Charli accompanied Logan to Stawell Hospital for his afternoon shift.

'Being in a medical environment seems to relax you,' he stated as they drove.

'Yes, it does. I guess as I can remember how to do medical procedures, it's a way for me to feel more in control of my present situation.'

He agreed. Both were silent for a while before Charli said, 'Logan…about that kiss…'

'Don't go there, Charli.' His words were abrupt and she

jerked back in surprise. 'Not now. Not while I'm driving. I'm desperately trying to concentrate so don't go talking about kisses when I'm working hard to ignore the way whatever perfume you're wearing is winding itself about my senses.'

'Oh.' A wave of longing spread through her at his words. She sniffed the air, not smelling anything except whatever aftershave *he* was wearing!

'And don't bite your lower lip in that cute way you're doing right now because it *really* distracts me.'

'Well, the same goes for you,' she countered. 'Stop saying I distract you because hearing that sets me on fire.'

Logan groaned as he pulled the car into the hospital car park and cut the engine. Silence filled the air. 'This is wrong, Charli.' He didn't turn to face her, he couldn't. If he looked at her, he would crumble. 'There are so many reasons why we shouldn't even be sitting here discussing this. You not knowing who you are is top of the list.'

'I know.'

'Good. Then it's settled. We're going to get out of the car and I'm going to pull superhuman control from somewhere and get on with my shift at the hospital.'

'Right.'

Neither of them moved. Slowly, Logan turned his head to look at her, knowing he should be getting out of the car instead. Charli glanced up at him, aware that the glazed look of desire in his eyes mirrored the one in hers.

'This is so wrong,' he whispered, as he leaned towards her.

'I know.' Charli held her breath, waiting impatiently for the moment when their lips would touch once more. It seemed like days, weeks, months since they'd been this close, instead of just a few hours.

When his mouth finally made contact with hers, she sighed with longing. She'd been following her instincts, trusting her instincts, and now those same instincts were telling her she'd never felt this way before.

She edged closer, frustrated to find she was bound by her seat belt, and as she wriggled, Logan quickly pulled back.

'Charli.' He cleared his throat.

'I guess I'm not your patient any more,' she stated.

'No. Definitely not. I discharged you hours ago, did I forget to tell you?' He shook his head and pressed his lips longingly to hers once more. 'No,' he said again. 'We need to go inside…*now*.' With that, he opened his door and stood, exhaling harshly as he raked a hand through his hair. He waited for her to climb out before locking the car and heading inside. He knew exactly where she was, he could feel her, sense her, and just knowing that was enough to send his mind into a spinning vortex of 'if onlys'. If only she didn't have amnesia, if only she would stay in Australia, if only she could be content to stay and live in Halls Gap with him.

'Too many issues,' he growled as he headed for the ward, Charli about a step behind him. He checked on Angie and was pleased to see she was feeling much better.

'We're going to need to monitor you quite closely from now on, at least until you get to learn the signs and symptoms of the angina attacks.'

'So this is going to happen again?' Angie asked, concerned.

'More than likely,' Logan responded. 'We'll work together, Angie. You, me, your family. This is something we're all involved in and you need to know you're not alone. We also need to talk about your daughter and the fact that her leaving next year is putting you under a great deal of emotional stress.'

'You think that's what brought on that pain yesterday?'

'I'm almost certain of it. I know it can't be easy to let go and, believe me, I'm not looking forward to it at all. As far as I'm concerned, both Trinity and Owen are living at home with me until they're well into their fifties. *Then* I might think about letting them go.'

Angie smiled at his words. 'Can I go home today?'

'I'd like you to stay until tomorrow morning just so we can monitor you for that extra twenty-four hours.'

'OK.'

'Good.'

Maree came into the room and called him over. 'You have two patients in A and E.'

'Thanks.' He looked at his patient. 'You take it easy and try to relax. We'll get through this, all right?'

'Yes.' She nodded and gave him a watery smile.

He said goodbye to Angie and looked around the nurses' station. 'Where's Charli?'

'She's reading in the hospital library.'

He shrugged and headed down to A and E with Maree. 'What have you got for me?'

'One is for removal of ear wax and the other is for a child with a urinary tract infection.'

'Sounds peachy.' He set to work and ended up with several cases trickling in over the next few hours. He called his children, making sure they were home from school, doing their homework and behaving themselves for their grandparents. He put them on speaker phone while he wrote up some case notes.

'Josie's here, too,' Trinity said. 'Grandma's going to let her and Mikey stay while their mum and dad are away with Amelia. Isn't that cool?'

'I'm glad they're happy.'

'Grandma said Amelia was really sick. Is she going to be OK?'

'She should be, sweetheart. We'll know more tomorrow morning. Be good for Grandma and I'll come and give you a kiss when I get home.' Logan heard a noise behind him and turned to see Charli. He smiled but went back to his conversation.

'Can I sleep at Grandma's tonight? Please, Dad? Mikey and Owen can sleep at our house and I can stay here with Josie.' Trinity was pleading with all her might and it looked as though she already had everything worked out.

'I'll discuss it with Grandma. Put her on.'

Logan was conscious of Charli being in the room and able to hear everything that was being said. He glanced at her while he waited for his mother to come to the phone. Even in his sister-in-law's clothes, she still looked...untouchable. She held herself with a mixture of poise, determination and grace. She was way out of his league and he'd known that the first time he'd laid eyes on her. It wasn't just her intellect or looks but the fact that she came from a completely different world.

He was a single parent with two children in tow. Those were the words his ex-fiancée had used when she'd broken off their engagement five years ago. She'd been astounded that Logan had not only wanted to give up his lucrative city practice but that he'd actually wanted to move to Halls Gap to keep his niece and nephew in their familiar surroundings.

'Logan?' His mother's voice brought himself back to the present. He discussed the children's sleeping arrangements with his mother. 'Trin's a very empathetic little girl, Logan. She feels Josie's and Mikey's unease and knows this solution might make it better for them.'

'She's so much like Trev.'

'She's like *you*,' his mother said softly. 'Also…' Rose cleared her throat and sighed. 'Wil wants to talk to you or Charli. He has some information for her.'

'OK.' Logan looked at Charli and she met his gaze. The fear which had been missing for most of the day was back. She was so torn between wanting and not wanting to know. 'I'll give him a call. Gotta go, Mum. Kiss the kids for me.'

'All right. See you later tonight.'

Logan rang off, watching Charli. 'Do you want me to call Wil now?'

Charli shook her head. 'No. Let it wait.' She felt safe here, safe with Logan, but finding out about herself had to remain her primary focus. She couldn't go on living her life in limbo. Although it had only been yesterday morning she'd been found, the time since then had been interesting. She'd discovered a lot about herself and for some strange reason she knew it was stuff she'd never realised before. Intuition was her guiding force and she was learning to listen to it. Still, she'd rather wait a little longer.

'Sure.' He nodded, not wanting to push her. Instead, he forced himself to turn his attention back to his work. He picked up his pen and started writing up another set of case notes.

Charli sat in the chair beside him. 'You think I'm wrong, don't you?' she said.

'No. I think you need to do what you need to do. If you want to prolong it for a bit longer, that's fine so long as you know it's there, waiting to be dealt with.'

'I *do* know and I'm not running away from it.'

He smiled at her and closed the file in front of him. 'Of course you're not. You're not that type.'

'Meaning?'

'You're a doer, Charli. It's part of who you are. You see a job that needs doing and you get in there and do it. You don't spend your life procrastinating over every little thing. You wouldn't have got as far in life if you did.'

Charli appreciated his words and sighed, feeling the earlier tension leave her. 'You're a nice man, Logan.'

'So you've said before.'

'That's because it's true. You give and you give and you give—to your parents, your children, your patients and your friends. It's just one of the things I've noticed about you since we met yesterday.'

Logan shook his head. 'Hard to believe we've learnt so much about each other in such a short time.'

Charli smiled. 'I was thinking the same thing.' She leaned across and kissed his cheek. 'Thank you for giving to me.'

Logan met her gaze and shook his head.

'I shouldn't have done that, I know,' she said, as though reading his mind. Logan was opening his mouth to respond when Maree walked in. He turned to look at the nurse and one glance at her face told him that something was wrong.

'Emergency?' he asked.

Maree stared at him in surprise. 'How did you know?'

'You have one of those faces,' he joked, and Maree swatted at him playfully.

'The ranger's office has just called through. Three inexperienced bushwalkers failed to return at sunset. They've only just located them at Redman Bluff.'

'Retrieval?'

'Yes.' She handed him a piece of paper. 'This is where you need to head to. Go out in the ambulance so you'll have everything on tap if you need it.'

'Right.' He turned and looked at Charli. 'Let's go.'

CHAPTER FIVE

CHARLI fell into step beside Logan. 'Do you often do retrievals?' she asked as they headed out of the hospital.

'Yes.'

'What about the hospital? Aren't you supposed to be on duty?'

'This hospital is split into two sections, medical and surgical. As I've been trained in retrieval techniques, it's better that I go. One of the surgical interns will take care of A and E until I'm back.'

'A and E?'

'Accident and Emergency. Same as ER.'

'Right. So, you can do that? Just like that? No forms? No red tape? You can just head out on retrieval?'

'You got it.' He smiled as they headed out to the ambulance. 'A bit different from your large American hospitals, eh?'

'Very different.'

Logan found Bruce and they set off. Charli was sitting in between the two of them and his awareness of her sparked his hormones into overdrive. Just the feel of her thigh, pressing against his, was enough to knock him completely off balance. Focusing his mind on work, he worked hard to answer the questions Charli was asking about the district. How many callouts did the ambulance get? What type of retrievals had they been on? How did they cope with limited facilities at the hospital?

'You're almost as bad as Owen,' Logan said with a laugh. 'Asking questions, thirsty for knowledge. I wonder if you're like this all the time?'

Charli glanced at him and smiled sheepishly. It was then Logan realised she was as aware of him as he was of her and the questions were a way to keep her mind occupied. He decided to follow suit and ask her a few questions about her working environment.

'Doesn't working in a big hospital and having to always be aware of red tape, cost-effectiveness and so on bother you?'

'No. Actually, it doesn't. I have a good team beside me and have learned how to number-crunch to my advantage.'

The instant the words were out of her mouth, Charli gasped and put her hand over her mouth. Logan smiled.

'There's another bit of information to file away about you. You know how to dwiddle the numbers.'

'I never said that and I don't even know what dwiddle means, you crazy Australian.' She giggled with delight, like a child unwrapping another layer of a large present. How did he do it? How did he know the right time to ask questions and get answers to come automatically out of her mouth? Was it Logan…or was she starting to remember more? She frowned and thought hard. While she'd been speaking to Logan, she'd been able to picture her office at the hospital, picture the accountant assigned to her department, picture her senior registrar. She thought harder—but she couldn't remember their names. She'd never been good at names. Numbers, statistics, surgical methods—not a problem. But names? Forget it… And she often did. She smiled, pleased she'd remembered something else about herself, and this time she'd remembered without prompting!

Bruce was starting to slow down and she realised they'd arrived at their destination. She noticed a police car was parked beside a ranger four-wheel-drive.

'Is that Wil's car?'

'Sure is.' Logan waited for Bruce to stop the ambulance before he climbed out, holding the door for Charli. 'Who's the ranger on duty, Bruce?'

'Tom,' he answered.

'Good. Tom's got a good head on his shoulders.'

Bruce radioed Tom to get directions to the bushwalkers' location. Tom radioed back what injuries he'd found on one of the men. 'Halley and Max are on their way out as well,' Tom's voice said through the UHF radio.

'Reinforcements are always good.' Logan smiled at Charli and she had to force her mind back into medical mode—it was the only part of her life she was one hundred per cent certain of. Helping Logan today had helped her immensely and now she had the opportunity to use her skills to help other people.

They climbed into retrieval overalls, put on helmets with lights attached and sorted out who was carrying which medical supplies. She was glad that, whatever had been happening in her life before yesterday morning, she'd worn decent lace-up shoes. It helped when she had to follow in Bruce's footsteps— Logan behind her—as they made their way down to where their patients were.

'Not too much farther,' Logan said as they started to descend into a small gorge.

'I now know why you have all your medical supplies in backpacks,' Charli muttered as she placed her hand on a rock to steady her descent.

Logan chuckled behind her. 'A different way of life. That's one of the things I love about being out here. You need your wits about you the whole time.'

'Are you saying you improvise with your medical care?'

'When the need arises, yes.'

She glanced over her shoulder at him, surprised but pleased at the same time.

'What? You *don't* improvise from time to time? Even in the big city?'

Charli smiled and turned back to concentrate on what she was doing. 'I think every doctor needs to, to a certain extent, but a few of my colleagues are strictly by-the-book people.'

'That's not always a bad thing.'

'I'm glad you said that, Logan, because I think *I'm* one of those people.'

Logan chuckled at her words and she wished he hadn't. The sound washed over her in glorious waves of happiness. She felt as though she could talk to him about anything.

'They should be around here.' Logan stopped, cupped his hands around his mouth. *'Cooee!'* he called, then waited.

'Cooee!' came an answering call.

'This way,' he said.

'Why didn't you just use the radio?'

'No need. We can pinpoint from following the direction the sound came from. They'll also know where we are and how much closer we're getting.'

'Oh.' Charli thought it through and realised it made sense. A few minutes later, Wil came through a thick clump of trees, almost scaring her. She jumped back and felt Logan's arms go about her waist to steady her. Charli gasped.

'Er…sorry…Charli. Didn't mean to scare you,' Wil apologised.

She sucked in air to her lungs, desperately trying to steady her heartbeat, which had nothing to do with Wil startling her and everything to do with Logan's touch. An overpowering shock had travelled through her body, leaving her slightly breathless. She edged away and he dropped his hands, but it took a few minutes after they'd moved on, back the way Wil had come, before her heartrate returned to almost normal.

They finally arrived where the first bushwalker had gone over. Wil and Tom had set up lights to illuminate the area. Tom was busy rigging up extra abseiling ropes to a stretcher, which was attached to what looked like a small crane.

'Ah, the cavalry has arrived.'

Logan introduced him to Charli and Tom set about briefing them.

'Three bushwalkers set out late this afternoon for a walk out here to Redman Bluff. Unfortunately, it appears they weren't too experienced and didn't take the proper precautions. The ranger helicopter found them after the alarm was raised when they didn't return to their camping ground. All three have gone over the bluff. Two are on the same ledge, the third is on a lower level. Max and Halley are on their way out and will probably be in time to take the first two casualties off your hands,' he said to Logan.

'Good.'

'We'll get you hooked up to a harness and then attached to the Larkin frame here.' Tom put his hand on the small winch.

'Once you're in, we'll send you down to assess the first two patients.'

Logan turned to Charli. 'Ever done any abseiling before?' He grinned when she gave him a nudge.

'Logan, how would I know?'

'Sometimes I ask the question and you know the answer, sweetheart. I was just trying it this time around. How do you feel about going over the cliff? Would you rather stay up here?'

Charli looked at the edge and felt instant dread.

'By that look, I think you'd be best to stay up top.'

'No.' She shook her head, the words 'believe in yourself' running through her mind. 'I... If you need me, I'll come down.'

Logan nodded and climbed into a harness, waiting while Tom hooked him up to the Larkin frame. With his backpack on, his safety helmet to shine light on what he was doing, Logan was lowered over the cliff.

Charli couldn't believe what she was seeing and wondered whether her heart had stopped beating at the sight of him disappearing from view. His smile was the only thing that reassured her. He'd probably done this a thousand times before so there was really no need for her to worry.

He called up to Tom that he was almost there and she realised he had a radio microphone so he could communicate with them.

'Little bit more. I'm almost on the first ledge...just dodging a tree. OK. I'm down. I can see them both.' He paused. 'One of them doesn't look good. Definite fractured arm, and that's just from looking at him.' Logan made his way over to the man and took his pulse. 'Patient one, pulse is thready.' He shifted over to where the second one lay. 'Patient two, pulse is stronger. He doesn't look to be too bad. Hey!' Logan called. 'Can you hear me?'

He received a muted response. 'He's rousing. Charli? I know you weren't too keen on coming down but it would be great if you could. Tom would do it but I need him up top to control the Larkin frame. Wil and Bruce don't have the qualifications I need.'

There was silence and Charli felt the three guys up top staring at her. 'If you can't do it, say so,' Tom said. 'You'll be no good to Logan if you go down and are too scared to do anything.'

Charli thought and swallowed over the lump of fear in her throat. She knew Logan wouldn't have asked her to come down if he didn't really need her.

'OK.' She nodded and before she could change her mind, Tom was helping her into a harness and hooking her to the Larkin frame. He handed her a pair of gloves and a headset so they could communicate. Her medical backpack was on and no sooner had she blinked than she was being coached over the side of the gorge.

'You're on a winch so you don't need to worry about doing anything,' Tom told her in his brief but explicit instructions. 'Logan will be waiting at the bottom to guide you down. Just breathe deeply and relax.'

Charli had opened her mouth to respond but found that she couldn't, so she nodded instead. She wanted to close her eyes, to make this all go away, but Tom had said if she did that she might get dizzy and that was the last thing she needed.

It seemed to take for ever yet at the same time not long at all before she felt Logan's hands guiding her in as she came to stand on the ledge beside him. 'OK, she's down.' Charli clung to him for a moment, knowing if she didn't she'd lose her nerve, and that was the one thing she'd vowed not to do.

'You did great, Charli. Just great.' Logan took off his helmet and bent his head to kiss her firmly. 'Now.' He replaced his helmet. 'We need to get to work.' He unhooked his rope. 'Send down the stretcher next, Tom.'

'Logan! What if you fall?'

He grinned at her. 'I won't. Come over here.' He helped her off with her backpack and pulled out a pair of surgical gloves. 'This is patient one. His pulse isn't good and...' He pointed. 'Look at that arm. Definitely broken. Can you work on him while I get this other guy organised?'

'Sure.' Charli pulled the backpack closer to her and swapped her gloves over. The ledge was wider than she'd anticipated and she was extremely grateful for that. She checked the man's pupils, BP, temperature and respiratory rate, calling out her findings to Logan and the others above. She secured a cervical collar around the patient's neck, silently apologising for the discomfort of the thing. 'His BP is dropping quite quickly. He has to be bleeding somewhere.' She ran her hands over her patient and found a large gash across his abdomen beneath his torn clothing.

She pulled on the fabric so she could access the area better. 'How are you doing, Logan?' The stretcher was almost down. 'Let me know if you need any help.'

'OK. How's patient one?'

'Bleeding. I need some sutures.'

'I'll get some out for you.' Logan dug in his backpack and pulled out the equipment she needed, loading the needle into the locking forceps.

'I'll have to stitch in layers. This is quite deep.'

'Let's get him stabilised and once he's up top we can sort things out.'

'How's your guy?'

'In better shape. I'll get an IV going for you before I transfer patient number two to the stretcher.'

'He needs Haemacell.'

Logan rigged up the drip, hanging the bag on a long, thick stick he'd stuck in the ground. The stretcher was hanging above them, waiting for the all-clear, and Logan got it down and managed to roll his patient into it. After securing the straps, he called for the stretcher to go up.

'He's all right to go up by himself?'

'Yes. He's fractured his left tibia and fibula and has a large bump on his forehead as well as several scratches and bruises, but that's about it. He's had a very lucky escape. We're not too far from the top and the patient is conscious. Tom will have him soon. Besides, if I'd gone up with him, I'd have had to steal your rope and leave you here unprotected. Not good for your first time on retrieval.'

Charli had been busy while they'd been talking, debriding the wound so she could see properly to suture off the vessels doing damage. 'I need more light.'

Logan grabbed a torch from his backpack and held it for her, keeping a check on the patient's pulse while she worked. 'That's a neat line of stitches,' he told her.

'Really? I think it's quite messy.'

'You're a perfectionist, Charli. No two ways about it.'

Tom radioed down to say the first patient was at the top and that Max and Halley were about five minutes away.

'They'll be working for their living as soon as they arrive,' Logan told him. 'Send down the next stretcher when you're ready. This guy's almost available for transfer as well.' Logan checked his pulse again. 'Stronger than when I first checked it.'

Charli was almost finished. 'I can do without the light. Take his obs and we'll see how he's doing now.'

'BP's up, respiratory rate and temperature are still the same. It's rather chilly out here so let's get him up to the top.'

'Agreed.'

'And how about you? Are you cold?' he asked her quietly. 'I don't want you getting sick again.'

'Actually, I'm quite hot…probably from all the excitement and hard work.' Her gaze met his and he smiled.

'You're one in a million, Charli Summerfield.' He smiled at her and she was glad she was still hooked up to the ropes as her limbs turned to jelly.

'Hey, stop flirting and concentrate on what you're doing,' Tom said with a laugh. 'Stretcher is on its way down to you.'

Logan and Charli prepared their patient for transfer to the stretcher, being very careful of the arm, which was twisted at an odd angle. 'His shoulder is dislocated but I'm hesitant to put it back in case the neck of humerus is fractured. Radius and ulna are definitely broken.'

Logan nodded. 'We'll just have to position him as best we can.' When the patient was secured on the stretcher, Logan clipped Charli in beside it.

'What about you?'

'I'll be fine.'

'Max and Halley are here,' Tom called down.

'Go on up.' Logan said the words softly and radioed to Tom to start the winch once more. She was one in a million and the more time he spent with her, the more he didn't want her to be taken from his life—as he knew she would be. He thought she was the bravest woman in the world for allowing herself to be winched over the edge of the gorge at night to tend to a patient. It must have been terrifying for her, especially as it had been her first time. His first time had been at a training exercise during daylight, with Wil pretending to be the patient, and he'd been scared stiff.

He anxiously waited for radio confirmation that they were both at the top and breathed a sigh of relief when it came.

'I'm going to send Max down to the patient below, Logan, and then I'll send a rope down for you to join him,' Tom said.

'OK.' It was another ten minutes before Logan found himself on the next ledge down, with Max firmly in control of the situation. The two men had worked together in the past and were able to stabilise the patient quickly. They called for the stretcher and Logan went up with the patient.

At the top, he looked around for Charli and saw her in the back of the ambulance with the patient she'd worked on. Logan hurried over, briefly greeting Halley.

'BP's started to drop again.' He heard the urgency in her voice. 'He's bleeding somewhere else.' She looked at Logan. 'We need to get him to surgery, stat.'

'Don't worry about the other two patients,' Halley told them. 'Max and I can take care of them.'

'Great.' Logan stepped out of his harness and climbed into the ambulance. Bruce was getting into the driver's side and soon they were on their way back to Stawell. Logan pulled on another pair of gloves. Charli was already doing the man's vital signs and Logan felt the abdomen where she'd previously sutured. He grabbed a stethoscope and listened.

He handed the stethoscope to Charli and changed over the drip while she listened. 'It doesn't sound right, does it,' she stated rhetorically. 'Let's go in and see what we can find.'

They quickly prepped him and Logan put an amnesic drug into the drip to ensure their patient didn't regain consciousness during the procedure.

Charli made an incision and checked around. 'It's the spleen,' she said. 'It's ruptured. Suction.'

They managed to keep their patient stabilised and by the time they arrived at Stawell Hospital, their patient was in dire need of the expertise of the surgical team.

Charli breathed a sigh of relief when he was taken off their hands. 'I didn't need that.'

'What? Working hard in an ambulance, after traversing a cliff?' Logan smiled and put his arms around her, not caring in the slightest who saw them. 'You're brilliant, Charli.' She gazed up at him and he saw that she was completely exhausted.

'Come and have a seat for a while before we head back home.'

'Mmm. That sounds nice,' she sighed. She allowed herself to be led to the kitchenette and sat down, watching Logan make her a cup of coffee. 'Actually, is there any herbal tea?'

'Uh…' Logan searched the cupboards. 'Yes. Want a cup?'

'Yes, please.' Charli leaned her head back and closed her eyes. 'When I'm working late at night in my lab, I sneak downstairs to Dr Hansen's little kitchen and pinch some of his herbal teas. They're delicious.'

Logan chuckled. 'Why don't you just keep some in your lab?'

'My lab assistant doesn't like the smell of them. He has an over-sensitive nose. Dr Hansen doesn't mind. I think he buys them just for me sometimes.'

'He sounds like a nice friend.'

'He is.' Charli sighed again and Logan finished making her tea.

'Your memories are starting to flow more smoothly now.' Charli opened her eyes and looked at him as he placed her tea on the table.

'I think it's you. You're so easy to talk to. You know when to prod and when to back away.' She smiled at him and sipped at her tea. 'Nice.' Logan sat beside her and lifted her feet up onto his legs and began massaging one foot at a time. 'Mmm. You're good at helping people, Logan Hargraves, but it makes me wonder.'

'What?'

'You give and you give, but do you ever receive?'

'More than you could imagine,' he said with total conviction. 'Those kids have given me so much. The town of Halls Gap, the people, the patients, all of them, they've given me so much.'

'I think it's completely ingrained in you, part of your genetic make-up. You can't help but be nice to people.' She smothered a yawn. 'It's your MO. Logan—the knight in shining armour.' She giggled, her eyes beginning to close. 'Where's your horse?'

Logan merely smiled, glad she was so relaxed after such a stressful evening. Ten minutes later, Wil came in to find Charli snuggled down in her chair, sound asleep, her feet on Logan's lap.

'How's everything going?' Logan asked.

'Good. Halley and Max have taken the other two guys back to Heartfield and are happy to keep them there. How's your patient?'

'Still in Theatre.' Logan shook his head in wonderment as he gazed at the woman beside him. 'Charli was amazing, Wil.' Logan told him what had happened in the ambulance. 'She gave that guy a better chance to fight for his life.'

'How does that sit with her not being licensed to practise in this country?'

'You may want to check that out for me, but from what I can remember she may well be licensed. At the conference, while she was speaking, she made a comment about the differences in operating theatres here. She was here for a week before the conference so my guess is that she did some demonstration operating during that time.'

'So for her to do that—'

'She'd have to be licensed,' they both finished together.

Wil nodded. 'I'll look into it for you.' He gestured to Charli. 'Looks as though your modern-day heroine is waking up.'

Charli shifted, stretched and yawned before opening her eyes. When she realised that she had two men watching her she sat up, feeling very self-conscious. 'Sorry.'

'Don't be,' Logan said quickly.

Charli put her feet on the floor and raised her hands to her hair. Finding it messy, she quickly finger-combed her blonde locks and pulled them back into a neat ponytail. Logan was mesmerised, watching her graceful movements.

'So, Logan, have you called your mum?' Wil asked, breaking the silence.

Logan quickly looked to his friend. 'Hmm…ah… What?'

'Your mother? Have you called her?'

'You're about the sixth person to ask me that. Yes, I've called my mum.' He shook his head. 'When everyone asks me like that, it makes me feel as though I'm a mummy's boy who still lives at home at the ripe old age of thirty-three and needs to check in if he's going to stay out after dark!'

Charli chuckled. 'It does sound pretty bad, you have to admit, Logan.'

Logan shook his head as Wil joined in her laughter. 'Thankfully,' Wil added, 'everyone knows the *real* reason you need to let your parents know what's happening.' He looked at Charli. 'Our man here was the local hero when he stepped in to look after those children. Every woman in the district thought he was as good if not better than Superman.'

'All except one.' Logan raised his cup to his lips.

'Well, Barbara was hardly in this district, and don't tell me you're still pining for her.' Wil stared at him in amazement. 'From the few times I met her, Logan, I have to tell you my honest opinion of the woman was that she was a piranha.'

'Barbara the Piranha?' Charli glanced at Logan, trying to suppress a grin.

'Go ahead. Laugh all you want.' He drained his cup, placed it on the table and then leaned back in his chair, stretching. 'It was a long time ago.'

Charli watched the stretch with interest, the way his shirt pulled against his biceps and firm trapezius. She was only vaguely aware of what the two men were saying.

'Yeah, but, please, mate, tell me you're not still carrying a torch for her.'

'No way. That torch snuffed itself out long before Trev and Alison's accident. I just hadn't realised it. Women like that and I don't mix—that much I've learned. Besides, the past five years have been the most rewarding of my life.' He stood and collected their cups from the table. 'I'm a family man now and that's the way it's going to stay.'

'Whew.' Wil wiped imaginary sweat from his brow. 'I'm pleased to hear that—about Barbara, I mean. She was bad news.'

'I wouldn't go that far,' Logan said in mild defence. 'She was just a woman who knew her own mind and wasn't going to let anything divert her. She wanted to be a prominent doctor's wife and, as far as I know, she is. She married a guy I went to medical school with who's more content with the amount he charges his patients than actually caring about his patients.'

'What do you think, Charli?'

Charli switched her attention from watching Logan to his friend. 'Think? About…' She stopped and cleared her throat. 'About what?'

'About Logan and his non-existent love life,' Wil said. Logan glared daggers into his friend's back before glancing at Charli. Her eyes were wide with shock and he could also see the beginning spark of desire.

He needed to nip this in the bud—and quickly. 'You don't need to answer that,' he told Charli in an offhand manner. 'Wil only asks questions like that because his own love life is even more non-existent than mine, and he doesn't have the excuse of looking after children to fall back on.'

Wil shrugged. 'He's right, unfortunately. Got any friends who are single?' he asked Charli, and then cringed after he'd said the words. 'Uh…sorry, Charli. I forgot.'

'You and me both.' She stood and another yawn escaped her lips. 'Excuse me. I'm pretty beat but before I forget, Logan said you had some news for me.'

'Oh, yeah. With the emergency and everything, it slipped my mind.' Wil glanced at Logan and then back to Charli. 'You might want to sit down.'

'Is it *that* bad?'

'Uh…yeah.' Wil waited until she was seated and glanced at Logan again before he began. 'I've managed to trace your steps as far as Melbourne. Thanks to Logan, we knew you'd been at the medical conference last weekend. The hotel you stayed at have faxed me through the printout of your account. I have it at the police station if you'd like to have a look at it.'

'Is she still registered there? Her belongings, work papers, not to mention her passport must be somewhere.'

'That's where it gets strange. They said you'd checked out yesterday morning.'

'Yesterday was Tuesday. She was in Halls Gap well before six o'clock!'

'What time?' Charli's voice was quiet.

'It was done via the before-hours checkout. They didn't process it until after eight o'clock. They said the room you'd stayed in was vacant. No belongings or anything else were left.'

'What about the car hire?' Logan asked. This wasn't good news. If Charli's passport and belongings were missing…

The two men watched as Charli stood and started to pace up and down in the small room. 'You hired the car when you had first arrived in Melbourne over a week ago. Everything was paid up front.'

'Something's not right here,' she said.

'You've got that straight,' Logan agreed. 'Something is wrong, Charli, and the answer is in your amnesia.'

Charli looked at Wil. 'You said there was no sign of a struggle, no sign that I wasn't alone when I fell.'

'Which can only mean you were out walking alone.' It was

Logan who said the words. 'You need to walk when you're upset or agitated.' Charli stopped pacing and glared at him. Logan only raised an eyebrow as if to say, See?.

'Something was bothering you,' Wil said, taking a small notebook from the top pocket of his uniform. He found his pen and started to write things down. 'You had a hire car, started driving and ended up here. You needed to get control of your thoughts so you went for a walk.'

Both men looked at Charli. She shrugged. 'It's possible.'

Logan realised she was tired and they'd talked enough for the moment. 'Well, Dr Summerfield, regardless of how you ended up here, it's now time for you to get your beauty sleep.'

'Are you implying that I look awful?' she challenged him, glad for the lighter tone.

'I wouldn't dream of it.' He stood and pulled out his phone. 'I'll just send a text message to my mother on her cellphone so I don't wake the kids, and then we'll go.'

'OK. I'll visit the bathroom, first,' Charli said.

'I'll check on the patients.'

'I'll head off. Drive safely, you two.' Wil put his notebook away and headed out the door with a cheery wave. Logan finished sending the message to his mother and then studied his phone more closely.

When Charli returned, he said quickly, 'What was your apartment security code again?'

'Testing my anterograde memory, Doctor?'

'No. I know there's nothing wrong with that. I'm figuring out a clue.'

'Uh, 18,12,68,37,88,73,' she recited, amazed at how easily the code came to her.

'You like Tchaikovsky. Look.' He held out his cellphone. 'Look at the numbers in relation to the letters. The last four sets spell out "overture".'

Charli looked at the phone, then at Logan then back to the phone again. 'You're right!'

'Don't sound so surprised. I may not have your IQ level but I'm no dummy.'

She smiled at him. 'I never said you were.' She held his phone out to him. 'Pumpkin time?'

'Hmm?'

'It means time to go.' She giggled. 'You know, Cinderella leaving the ball at midnight because her carriage is going to turn into a pumpkin.'

'Oh *that* pumpkin time. Sure. I knew that's what you meant.'

She laughed as they headed out to check on the patients. 'I'm sure you've read the story to your kids quite a few times.'

'Try a few hundred,' he whispered as they entered the ward. He checked on the patients, wrote up some medication prescriptions in case they were needed and said good-night to the nursing staff.

When they walked out of the hospital, it was after midnight. Both were silent as they started the half-hour drive back to Halls Gap. Logan dug around in the console for a tape and finally found the one he wanted. He put it on and soon the strains of Tchaikovsky filled the air.

Charli felt herself instantly relax and her eyes began to close. 'Thank you,' she whispered.

Logan was surprised to hear her breathing turn deep so soon but he didn't blame her for wanting to sleep. She must be so annoyed and frustrated, not knowing who she was or what had happened to her. She was scared as well—he'd seen that in her eyes tonight when Wil had been talking. To combat it, she'd started to pace. Nervous energy.

Her memory needed time to heal. The book he'd borrowed from the hospital library detailed the symptoms of retrograde amnesia as well as hysterical amnesia. Physically, her head appeared to be all right. She had a bruise on her skull but that would heal. According to the textbook, she would start to remember the events leading up to her arrival in Halls Gap within two to three days of the initial incident, but as there was also an emotional trauma present, it might take months for it to heal. It was all a matter of unlocking what she'd been trying to suppress in the first place.

She started to twitch a little, which concerned Logan, but then he realised she was only dreaming. Then her breathing started to become fast and shallow and he realised the dream wasn't such a good one after all. As much as he wanted to wake her, he knew she needed to dream out the pain that was surrounding her. The question was, how much would she remember on waking?

He pulled the car into the driveway outside his house and, watching her closely, cut the engine.

As though on cue, Charli gasped and jerked upright. 'Chuck! *No!*' Her eyes were wide open but he wasn't sure she was seeing things clearly as she appeared to be groping around, fighting against the restraining seat belt.

'Charli?' he said softly, and she turned frightened eyes to him. She was still struggling against the seat belt so he pressed the release button.

Her breathing was harsh and for a few moments he wasn't sure she saw him—*really* saw him. Slowly, her breathing began to settle. 'Logan?' Her voice was a whisper. 'Logan, is that you?'

'Yes.' He touched her hand. 'It's me. Everything's all right.'

'No. No it's not. They're coming for me. They're after me.'

He watched her closely, wondering if he should tell her she'd called out Chuck's name. 'Who?' he tested.

'I don't know. I'm running…always running.' Tears had started to stream down her face and she was really trembling. Logan growled something inaudible and climbed from the car, stalking around to her side to help her out.

Once she was standing, he hauled her into his arms and held her close. 'Cry it out, sweetheart. Cry it out.'

It was then she began to sob. Her body was racked with spasm after spasm and he knew the worst thing was that she had no idea why. He knew he'd feel that way if the positions were reversed.

'Hold me. Hold me, Logan,' she whispered frantically against his shirt. He was cold, they both were, but he couldn't move. He gathered her closer, as close as he possibly could, his arms strong and firm about her.

The urge to protect this woman for the rest of his life was incredibly strong and Logan vowed then and there that if anyone tried to hurt her, they'd have to go through him first.

CHAPTER SIX

ONCE Charli had cried out all the tears and tension which had mounted to boiling point, Logan led her inside. His mother greeted them and when she saw that Charli was upset she whisked her away to the bedroom. Logan was deeply concerned for Charli but knew his mother's natural caring would help settle her for the night.

He raked a hand through his hair, exhaled harshly and worked desperately hard to get his body under control. Just holding Charli in his arms had been enough to send him almost over the top. So many emotions, so many feelings, and the surge of protectiveness hadn't helped.

He checked on the children, trying not to think about Charli. Owen and his friend Mikey were sleeping soundly, the covers strewn all over the place. He smiled and straightened the covers back over them, then checked the heater as it was going to be another cold night and he didn't want either of them to freeze. Then he headed into the kitchen.

He boiled the kettle, more for something to do rather than anything else. He was sitting at the bench, looking into his cup, thinking of how beautiful Charli was—the way small strands of hair would fly free in the breeze, the way her eyes twinkled when she smiled—when his mother came in.

'She's settled now. I made her take some paracetamol because she was bound to have a headache after crying like that.'

'You heard her?'

'I heard you pull up and was...curious as to why you didn't come straight in.' His mother gave him a contrite look. 'I looked out the window to make sure everything was all right. I swear, Logan. That's the only reason I looked. I wasn't snooping.'

He smiled. 'It's all right, Mum.'

'You were good to let her cry it out.' Rose shook her head. 'She's very fragile.'

'That's understandable.'

'I mean it, Logan. She's *very* fragile.' Rose gave him a pointed look and Logan raked his hand through his hair and stood.

'I know, Mum. Don't you think I know that?'

'Yet you're attracted to her.'

'Yes. She's an incredible woman.'

'What you know of her,' Rose added.

'Yes.' Logan shook his head and crossed his arms. 'What a mess,' he mumbled.

Rose came over and stretched up to kiss her son. 'You're a good man, Logan.' She touched his cheek tenderly. 'It's your greatest strength…and your greatest weakness. Try and get some sleep, son.'

Logan stood where he was as his mother let herself out of his house. He didn't move for a few minutes then tossed his drink down the sink, put his cup into the dishwasher and silently walked through the quiet, dark house.

He paused momentarily outside Charli's room, before calling on superhuman strength and continuing on to his bedroom.

Logan hardly slept that night, or the next, or the next. By Saturday morning, he woke with his sheets in a complete tangle and his head pounding. Usually on a Saturday both children came into his room, but not this morning. He glanced at the bedside clock and was surprised to find it was almost nine.

He stood, pulled on a pair of jeans and made his way through the house. 'Owen?' he called. 'Trin? Come on, kids, wake up. You've got a soccer game in an hour and a half.' He opened Owen's bedroom door while he was talking, only to be met by a messy bed but no child. He checked Trinity's room—the same situation.

Perhaps they were watching television. He headed to the living room but it, too, was empty. Frowning, Logan headed back towards his bedroom and it was when he was walking past Charli's room that he heard the squeal of a child's laughter.

He froze, then raised his hand to knock before opening the door. He saw Charli, lying in bed with two 'bumps' on either side of her beneath the covers. Her hair was wild and messy, her eyes were glowing with delight and her mouth was curved into the biggest, brightest smile he'd ever seen. How could one woman be so incredibly beautiful first thing in the morning?

Logan was lost.

His willpower was gone.

The internal war he'd been fighting since meeting her was lost.

He took a step into the room, not breaking eye contact, and saw the expression in her eyes turn from one of happy delight to overwhelming desire. His heart was pounding fiercely in his chest and his breathing was shallow.

The squirming and giggling of the two bodies beneath the covers were what stopped him.

He cleared his throat and closed his eyes for a moment, before saying, 'Where are my children? Have you seen them, Charli?'

'Uh…' She, too, cleared her throat. 'I have no idea.'

'I've checked their rooms, I've checked the living room because I thought they might be watching television but I can't seem to find them anywhere.'

There were more giggles from Owen, with Trinity shushing him up. Logan knew they were about to burst and so he knelt at the foot of the bed, reached out a hand and brought it down on their bodies.

'You appear to have some lumps in your bed, Charli. Let me get them out for you.' Logan began tickling his children and Charli started yelping with pain as little arms and legs went everywhere beneath the covers. Finally, they both came up for air, wide grins on their faces.

'We tricked you, Daddy,' Owen said.

'He knew where we were,' Trinity added, although the smile on her face was as wide as her brother's.

'I was wondering where you'd got to. I was waiting for my cuddles as I do every Saturday.'

Trinity shrugged. 'We thought Charli needed some, too, and she's never had Saturday cuddles before.'

Logan was amazed at the insight of his seven-year-old. 'You're quite right.'

'You could get into Charli's bed, too, Dad,' Owen said. 'Then we can all have a cuddle together.'

His innocent words were enough to make Logan's gaze swing to Charli's. Her gaze was wide and filled with shocked surprise at Owen's suggestion. Logan quickly stood and belatedly remembered to drag air into his lungs.

'That's OK, mate. I'm sure Charli's had enough for one morning. Come on, you two. Time to get up and get ready for soccer.'

'Aw, do we have to?' came the chorus from both of them. As they said the words, they instantly snuggled into Charli. Logan watched as she hesitantly placed an arm around both of them and hugged them close. She looked at him, her eyes beginning to fill with tears. She was…touched, he realised, and again wondered about her background.

'Charli's going to be coming to your game today. Don't you want to show her how well you can play?'

'Yeah!'

That got both of them moving and they were up and out of the bed, faster than he'd seen them move in a long time. 'Go get your kit on and I'll get your breakfast ready,' he called. Logan walked to the door and turned to look at the woman who'd been abandoned in the bed. 'Are you all right? Not too many bruises, I hope.'

Charli sniffed. 'I'm fine.' She reached across for a tissue and dabbed at her eyes. 'They're so…' She searched for the right word.

'Encompassing.' Logan nodded, knowing exactly how she felt. He gripped the door handle and tried not to clench his teeth. Now that it was just the two of them, the urge to take her in his arms and plunder her mouth was overpowering.

He cleared his throat again. 'I'd better go.' With that, he

turned and went out of her room, closing the door firmly behind him. He waited a beat before heading to the kitchen and focusing on what he needed to do.

Two hours later, they were at Stawell oval, sitting on fold-out chairs, cheering for their team. Wil was the coach and was busy calling instructions from the sidelines.

'He gets really involved in the games, doesn't he?' Charli observed to Logan.

'He comes across as this big, rough policeman and then you see him coaching these kids who really have no idea what they're doing, and you realise he's just a big softy.'

'You've been friends for a while?'

'Yes. We went to school together.'

'Were you raised in Halls Gap?'

'No. Inner suburb of Melbourne. But we came to the Grampians for holidays almost every year. Sometimes Wil came with us and we all fell in love with the area. My parents decided to retire here and when Trev came to visit them on holiday he met Alison, who was a Grampians native, and ended up staying.'

Sadness had crept into his voice when he'd mentioned his brother. 'You were close?'

'Yes. Very. Trev was always there to support me, or to kick my butt, if need be.'

Charli smiled. 'Did he do that often?'

'He did it about two months before he died. Told me I'd turned into a snob and to dig deep to find out who I was again before I lost myself completely.'

'Harsh.'

'But necessary. He was right. I'd got stuck on the money-go-round.'

'Barbara?'

Logan laughed. 'Yes. I don't blame Barbara, it's just who she is. She was my practice manager and she'd get annoyed with me when I spent too much time with my patients. She said it wasn't cost-effective. I came here for a break and Trev told me to take a good look at who she was because he certainly didn't want her for a sister-in-law.'

Charli shook her head. 'He must really have loved you to talk like that.'

'He did.' Logan nodded. 'He did.'

'My brother died when I was twelve.'

'Chuck?' Logan said the name hesitantly, not wanting to break her train of thought, but it was becoming more and more urgent to find out exactly who Chuck was. He still hadn't told Charli about the other night when she'd had that bad dream in the car, although he'd mentioned it to Wil.

Wil had been working overtime, trying to piece together the set of events that had brought Charli into their lives. No contact had been made with her mother and Wil had contacted the police in Los Angeles to try and discover Catherine Summerfield's whereabouts.

'I don't like it that something seems to have happened to Charli's mother, as well as her,' Wil had said to Logan on the phone.

'Coincidence?' Logan had asked.

'I'm not too sure. There's nothing on this Chuck fellow you've mentioned but I'm still looking into it.' Wil had paused. 'You'll let Charli know?'

'Yes,' Logan had agreed, concerned about Charli's mental health. Still, she had the right to know. She'd taken the news well but he'd seen the worry in her eyes. That's why he was so thankful for today. The sunshine, the soccer match—it was all an escape from the unanswered questions that surrounded them.

'Chuck?' The name didn't sound foreign on her lips and she thought for a moment. 'No. His name was Eddie. My father left not long after his death and my mother focused her attention on me.' Charli shook her head as the memories poured out once more. 'That's amazing.' She looked at Logan. 'Just like that, the words come out and the memory is there.'

He smiled. 'You'll find that happening more often now.'

'I know. That's what the text said would happen but a part of me doubted it.'

Logan took her hand in his and gave it a little squeeze,

before quickly letting go. Charli glanced over at him, the smile fading from her face.

'It's electric, isn't it?' she whispered.

He didn't pretend he didn't know what she was talking about. 'Yes.' Logan cleared his throat, feeling highly uncomfortable.

'Do you think we'll be able to control it?'

Logan took off his hat and raked a hand through his hair, glad he was wearing his sunglasses so she couldn't see his eyes. 'We have to. It isn't going to do either of us any good.'

'Logically, I agree, but you have to understand, Logan, that all I have to go on at the moment are my emotions. I'm stuck here, at least for the next three weeks until something can be done about getting me a new passport.'

'I can't believe it takes that long.'

'That's what Wil said the American Consulate said.'

'I'm surprised he hasn't been able to contact your mother.'

'I know. It scares me a little. What if something's happened to her, too?'

'Is that what you think? Is that what your instincts tell you?'

'Yes, and I just hope I'm wrong.'

He turned and looked at her, noticing she'd shifted her sunglasses down off her head to shade her own eyes. She was wearing a pair of navy shorts, which revealed far too much of her gorgeous legs, and a white cotton shirt. The gold loveheart chain was absent from her neck and he wondered if she had remembered something about Chuck but wasn't willing to tell him.

An old sun hat of his mother's was on her head and she looked relaxed, comfortable—and as though she belonged here. Now was not the time to bring up the subject of the mysterious Chuck.

A thud and then a loud scream snapped his thoughts back to reality and he realised that one of the players had been injured. Wil was waving his arms, motioning to Logan.

'Looks like we're on,' he told Charli, grabbing the first-aid kit and heading over. 'What's the problem?'

'Cameron's leg is sore,' almost every other player told him.

'He scored the goal and then he got hurt,' Owen said jubilantly. 'Yahoo. Way to go, Cam.'

'Is he going to be all right, Daddy?' Trinity was crouching beside her father, concern on her face.

'Let me have a look.' Logan checked the six-year-old over, making sure his eyes were fine. His pulse rate was elevated, but that was to be expected. Then Logan carefully felt the boy's right leg. Cameron was really crying, his mother leaving her post at the drinks table to rush over.

'What is it, Logan? What's happened?' she asked urgently.

'Ambulance?' Wil asked.

'Yes, thanks, Wil. It feels as though he's broken his leg. I'd like to get him up to the hospital for an X-ray and we'll take it from there.'

'Does he need surgery? Will he be all right?'

'It doesn't *feel* as though it's bad. Probably a cast will do the trick but I can't say for sure until I've seen the X-rays.'

'Why can't you tell now?' Cameron wailed.

'Because I'm not Superman, mate. I wish I *did* have X-ray vision because it would certainly save the hospital a lot of time and money.' Logan carefully lifted the boy into his arms.

'You're as strong as Superman,' Cameron said, and Logan grinned at him, glad his tears were decreasing.

'It's very nice of you to say so,' he told him.

'Do I get to go in an ambulance?'

'You most certainly do. I'm just going to splint your leg so we can get you out of the way and the game can continue. You don't want to have a soccer ball rolling around you while you're lying in the middle of the field, do you?'

Cameron shook his head. 'Then everyone might stand on me as well.'

'You don't want that.'

'No, I don't want that,' Cameron agreed.

Logan put him down on one of the benches and had a better look at his leg. Charli came over and introduced herself to Cameron and his mother.

'Oh, we know who *you* are, dear,' his mother said. 'Everyone does. You're the talk of the district.'

'Feels as though his right tib and fib are fractured.'

Charli felt Cameron's leg. 'Greenstick.'

'Yes.'

'And you scored such a fantastic goal,' she said to Cameron. 'Well done.'

'You talk funny.'

'Cameron!' his mother scolded.

Charli smiled. 'I guess I do, but to me it's all of *you* who sound funny.'

Cameron laughed and swallowed some medicine Logan gave him.

As the hospital was only a few blocks away, Bruce arrived with the ambulance in next to no time. Cameron was feeling much better and was disappointed he couldn't stay and watch the end of the game.

'I think he's going to be as right as rain,' Logan told the boy's mother as they climbed into the ambulance beside the boy. When they arrived at the hospital, Cameron was taken for X-rays and, as Logan had suspected, the diagnosis came back as a greenstick fracture to the tibia.

'What's that?' his mother asked.

'It's when the fracture is incomplete. If you look here at the X-rays…' Logan held them up for her '…you'll see that the bone is bent on one side and splintered on the other.'

'Oh, yes. What's next?'

'As the fracture hasn't broken the skin, we can realign the bone and put a cast on his leg. He'll be on crutches for at least four weeks. Then I'll do a check X-ray to make sure everything is healing all right, and after that he'll have a splint on for a few more weeks.'

'And that's it? Apart from that, he's all right?'

'Yes.'

'So no more soccer?'

'No, not for the rest of the season.'

'I'm glad he scored that goal, then.' She laughed.

'So am I. Poor Wil, though. With Mikey and Josie going to Melbourne to be closer to their sister, and now Cameron, his team members are dropping like flies.'

'He'll cope,' Cameron's mother said. 'He always does.'

'OK. Well, let's get this under way so we can all celebrate the soccer team's big win.'

Thankfully, Cameron enjoyed the sensation of the wet, gooey plaster being slathered onto his leg and sat still long enough for Logan to get the cast on.

When it was dry, they found him some small crutches and Logan showed him how to use them, making Cameron squeal with peals of laughter as the crutches were way too small for the six-foot-three-inch doctor.

Logan wrote up the discharge notes and went in search of Charli. She was in A and E, talking to Maree. 'Ready?'

'Sure am.'

He looked around him. 'Where are the kids?'

'Wil took them home,' Charli told him. 'They were so bouncy and full of excitement that there was no way Owen was going to sit still.'

'OK. Then I guess we're ready to go. Thanks, Maree.' Logan nodded to the nurse as he escorted Charli out. She handed him his hat and sunglasses before putting hers on. It was just after one o'clock and Logan felt his stomach grumble. 'You hungry?'

'Sure am.'

'Seems to be your standard answer at the moment.' Logan set off down the street towards the shops. 'How about a hamburger? Or is that too American for you? Meat pie and sauce?'

Charli laughed. 'After being winched over a cliff, I'm game to try anything new. Meat pie and sauce sounds…neat.'

Logan couldn't help smiling. 'That's tomato sauce,' he clarified. 'Not gravy or anything else.'

'Oh.' She considered it for a moment. 'That's still all right.'

'We'll have to get some other Australian foods for you to try while you're here.'

'Such as?' As she was walking, her hand brushed against his and she felt a current buzz up her arm, making her gasp. Logan turned to look at her, the smile slowly sliding off his face. He dragged in a deep breath and clenched his jaw. He tried to get his brain to work, to compile an answer to her question, but all he could think about was touching her, holding her hand, letting her know she was becoming vitally important to him.

'I can't do this,' he mumbled.

'What?' Charli's heart was pounding fiercely in her chest. She kept walking, keeping pace with him as they continued.

Logan shook his head again and reached down to grasp her hand. Charli jumped at the contact and stopped walking. 'Sorry.' He loosened his grip and she realised he'd misinterpreted her body language.

'No. Don't let go.' The words tumbled out of her mouth in a rush as she squeezed his hand tighter.

'I didn't mean to startle you. I just…' He raked his free hand through his hair again. 'I just needed to touch you.'

Charli smiled at him. 'I know the feeling.'

'We probably shouldn't—'

'But we are,' she finished for him, and started walking again. 'Now, let's find me some Aussie food to try.'

'You got it, mate.' Logan tightened his grip on her hand, wondering if he'd ever be able to let go. In the next block down, he led them to a take-away, and as they went inside he dropped her hand and removed his sunglasses. 'G'day, Cedric. How's business been today?'

'Quite good, mate. Quite good. What can I get ya?'

'Two pies with sauce.' Logan peered at the cakes. 'Got any lamingtons?'

'I'll just check with the missus.' Cedric disappeared out the back for a moment while Charli perused the large fridge full of drinks.

'So, is there a typical Aussie drink I need to try or can I just opt for a cola?'

Logan grinned and the effect went straight to her heart. 'Whatever you like. Grab one for me as well.'

'We do have some lamingtons,' Cedric announced on his return. 'Two?'

'That'd be beaut, mate.' A few minutes later, their lunch in paper bags, they headed out of Cedric's store. Charli was pleased when Logan managed to juggle their purchases so he could take her hand in his once more as they headed back to the soccer oval.

It was now deserted and he led them to a bench and reluctantly let go of her hand. 'Take a load off,' he said as he straddled the seat, placing his lunch before him. Charli did the same, sitting opposite him, and was pleased when she caught him sneaking a glance at her legs.

He took the pie out of the bag, then the sauce satchet. He squeezed the sauce on top of the pie pastry, watching as Charli mimicked his actions.

'So what's inside?'

'Probably better if you don't ask,' he said with a laugh. 'Meat with gravy.'

'And you put tomato sauce on top?'

'Sure do, ma'am,' he said in an American accent.

'Are you making fun of me?'

'Sure am, ma'am.'

Charli could only grin and watched closely as he raised the pie to his mouth and took a large bite. She took a deep breath and followed suit. 'Here goes.' She took a bite, the sauce going over her upper lip, a few flakes of pastry falling down onto her top and the hotness of the meat inside mildly burning her tongue.

Logan swallowed and then cheered as she licked her top lip. 'We'll make an Aussie out of you yet, Dr Summerfield. What do you think?'

She swallowed. 'About being made into an Aussie or the pie?'

'Let's start with the pie.'

'Not bad. Not bad at all. It's spicier than I thought it would be.' She took another bite, chewed and swallowed. 'In fact, it's quite good. Is there any more sauce, or *real* ketchup for that matter?'

He pulled another sauce satchel from his bag. 'I always get a spare.'

'My hero.'

They ate their pies, grinning at each other before moving on to the cake covered with chocolate syrup and coconut.

'Now, lamingtons I could get to love,' she mumbled through her mouthful, bits of coconut flying.

Logan laughed. 'You're all class.'

Charli swallowed. 'I can't explain it, Logan. I feel so…so…free. It's wonderful.'

'Pies and lamingtons! Who knew that's what it would take for you to feel that way.'

'It's not just them and you know it.' She ate her last mouthful and had a drink. Logan stood and disposed of their litter before returning to his seat.

'What is it then?'

'Pardon?'

'If it's not the food, what else is it that makes you feel free?'

'Fishing?'

A slow smile spread across his face. 'Perhaps. Are you going to bite?'

'You? Only if you're good.'

'Charli!' Logan was a little shocked and surprised at her attitude. 'The woman I met at the conference last weekend would never have said anything like that.'

'How would you know? Did you know me that well?'

'No.' He reached out to brush a strand of hair from her face. He tucked it behind her ear and began to caress her cheek.

'So what gives you the impression I'm behaving out of character?' She took his hand in hers and raised it to her mouth, carefully kissing each knuckle.

Logan sucked a breath in. 'Well, you didn't do *that*, for starters.'

'Does it bother you?'

'Very much so.' Her gaze flew to meet his. 'But in a good way.' His heart rate had increased and he knew she could see the desire in his eyes.

'Why haven't you kissed me?'

Her question only served to add more fuel to the fire that was now raging within him.

'Because I knew I wouldn't be able to stop.'

Slowly she nodded her head. 'What a shame you have such a good answer.'

'Why?'

'Because it makes it impossible for me to hold a grudge against you.'

'I'm glad to hear that.'

She watched his throat as he swallowed, wanting to press her lips to his Adam's apple.

Logan groaned. 'Don't look at me like that.'

'Like what?' The two words were whispered as she edged closer to him.

'Like you're ready to devour me, like you did that lamington.'

'And if I am?'

Logan pushed a shaky hand through his hair and shuddered. 'We can't!' His self-control was almost at breaking point.

'I know, I know. It's insane. We're setting ourselves up for future hurt. I understand all that and so do you.'

'I have two children to think about.' He said the words, hoping they'd have the effect of a bucket of cold water, but Charli was still moving in, her gaze flicking between his eyes and his lips.

'I know, and you're a great father, Logan. It's just another one of the things I like about you.'

'You like that?' He shook his head in astonishment. 'You are full of surprises.'

'Are you going to keep stalling or are you going to kiss me.' It was a statement, not a question, as he was positive she already knew the answer.

CHAPTER SEVEN

LOGAN knew that actions spoke louder than words and so, instead of stalling any longer, he tenderly brushed his lips across hers.

'How was that?'

Charli's gaze met his as she pretended to think for a second. 'Nice, but not quite what I had in mind.'

'Oh. So you were hoping for something more like *this*?' Again, Logan lowered his mouth to hers, one hand sliding around her neck to fist in her hair, holding her head in place. Again he brushed his lips across hers, testing, tasting...teasing. Sweet, slow torture. That's what he wanted to do to her *and* to himself. He wanted this moment to last for ever, to be permanently burned on his brain. Two, three more times, he pressed his lips to hers.

The fourth time, he edged his tongue between the softness of her lips and was rewarded with a small gasp from her. Power at the pleasure he could give her soared through him and he continued his attack—his planned, calculated and careful attack.

Charli had never been kissed this way before in all of her thirty-one years. The fact that she had no memory of those thirty-one years made no difference at all. She was *positive* she'd never been kissed this way before. She felt it deep down inside and as his lips moved over hers, she opened her mouth to him, wanting to drug his senses as much as he was drugging hers.

She had no idea how much longer she could take this unbelievably pleasurable, sweet torture. It was as though a spring was winding itself ever so slowly and she knew she was almost at the point where she was about to explode.

Again, his tongue slipped between her lips, teasing her. Her breathing was hard and fast, her heart was pounding fiercely against her ribs and she felt decidedly light-headed. Swooning! She was actually swooning.

She pulled back for a second to drag a shaky breath into her lungs, her eyelids heavy and unable to open.

'You all right?' The words were whispered near her ear as he pressed kisses to her cheek. He then worked his way around, nibbling her earlobe and again she gasped—a flood of goose bumps cascading over her. She shivered slightly and he shifted in closer, his fingers at her nape making small soothing circles.

'Hmm.' She rested her head on his shoulder.

'Are you going to sleep?' he asked, the deep resonance of his voice washing over her.

'No. I wouldn't dare miss whatever is coming next. I'm just so…relaxed. I can't believe it. My eyes feel like lead.' She sighed. 'How do you do it? How do you make me feel so calm and comfortable when only moments ago—' She broke off as a yawn escaped her. 'See?' She leaned back so she could look at him. 'How?'

'Endorphins.' He watched her for a moment. 'Come on. I'll take you home.'

'No!' The word came out faster than she'd anticipated. 'Let's just stay a bit longer. I think you need to kiss me again.'

Logan eased back a little and slowly shook his head. 'I don't know if that's safe.' His words made her smile, which only made matters worse for him.

'Kiss me, Logan.'

He groaned and brought his mouth down to meet hers once more. Again he teased and tantalised her lips but this time she was ready for the sensations. Instead of being surprised, she welcomed them, and after a few seconds of sweet torture she found she couldn't take it any longer.

Shifting closer, she plunged her fingers into his hair and moved her mouth over his in an intimate but demanding manner. He stilled—for a fraction of a second—before the heat flooded through him and he met her enthusiasm head on.

His control had snapped. *She* had snapped it! He couldn't believe how incredible she was—exotic and unique—and he knew he was hooked. His mouth moved hungrily over hers, their needs evident, their passions mutual, their desire burning out of control.

It was as though he'd been in a drought all his life and now, by some miracle, the rains had come and he was alive once more. Nothing mattered. Nothing, except the two of them. The rest of the world fell away as he gave in to emotions which had been dormant for years and others which had never seen the light of day.

The need to keep her with him, the small spark which had begun only a few days ago when they'd met, was now a raging bush-fire burning out of control, and there was nothing at all he could do—and he didn't want to—to put it out.

She knew she'd be able to break his control and a surge of feminine power passed through her, quickly followed by a feeling so foreign to her she gasped. He wasn't the only one out of control. Her mind was racing, trying to process everything, focus on every emotion she felt, and it was all starting to get too much for her.

She'd dreamt about him kissing her but there was no way her dreams had matched what was happening right now. If she'd thought herself breathless before, it was nothing compared to now. Her heart hammered out a tattoo as she gave everything she had to the kiss.

As she leaned in closer, her mild scent continuing to wind its way about him, he didn't think this moment would ever end. She tasted of sweetness and sunshine and everything good, and he knew then and there that he was addicted.

Finally, it became too much for both of them and they broke away at the same time, dragging air into their lungs. Neither was able to speak for quite some time, Charli resting her head on Logan's shoulder, Logan resting his head against hers.

'You all right?' he murmured, and shifted back so she could lift her head.

'Hmm?' She gazed up at him and then whispered, 'Wow!'

His smile captivated her. 'My sentiments exactly. When we can move, I think it's time for us to head back to reality.'

'Do we have to?'

Logan looked down into her beautiful face, once more mesmerised by her. There was sadness in his tone as he said, 'Yes.' For the first time in five years he felt resentful of his responsibilities. Not only the children but his private practice, his work here in Stawell at the hospital. Right now he wanted it all to go away, for there just to be Charli and himself, and that train of thought surprised him.

He stood and tugged Charli to her feet. Neither of them spoke as they walked hand in hand to the car. On the drive he noticed her eyelids begin to droop and soon she was snoozing. He didn't blame her. He wouldn't have minded a bit of a kip himself.

He was just pulling into the driveway when Charli sat bolt upright and spouted off a large number.

'Where did *that* come from?' Logan was astonished.

'I have no idea.'

He scrambled around in the car for a piece of paper and pen. 'Say it again.'

Charli repeated the number.

'That's a fifteen-digit number. Do you know what it's for?'

Charli thought hard. 'No.'

Logan reached into his pocket and pulled out his cellphone. He wrote down the corresponding letters to the number. 'Something's not right.' He looked at it again. 'Oh, I get it. You've used text shorthand for the word "your".'

'Well, what is it?' Her impatience was mounting.

'Believe in urself.' He looked at Charli. 'Does this mean something to you?'

'I don't know. I mean, it's what I keep telling myself over and over, to believe in myself.'

'Why do you remember everything in numbers, rather than just the phrase?'

'I'm left-brained.'

'Pardon?' Logan frowned at her.

'I'm more left-brained than right-brained. As a general rule, people who are excessively one or the other think differently. Right-brained people—creative types—are more likely to remember in pictures. Left-brained people—logical types—are more likely to remember in numbers.' She shrugged.

'But where did "Believe in urself" come from?'

'I don't know.' Charli closed her eyes, willing her brain to co-operate, and amazingly she had another brief flash of memory. It was of a wall with a Monet painting on it. She thought hard but she couldn't unlock anything else.

Logan watched her. 'Leave it, Charli.' He took her hand in his and gave it a gentle squeeze. 'It'll come.'

She opened her eyes and sighed with frustration. 'But I'm so close. I can see a Monet picture on a wall but I don't know where the wall is.'

'Perhaps there's a safe behind the picture and the number is the combination for it.'

'That's what I was thinking.'

'What's in the safe?' Logan pondered.

'Good question.'

He shifted in his seat to look at her. 'It makes you uneasy.'

'Yes. I don't know what it is…I just get a bad feeling about it.'

Logan let go of her hand and placed his hand on her shoulder. 'Whatever it is, I'm here to help you, Charli. I'm on your side.'

'I know.' She gave him a shaky smile and he felt himself weakening. Logan slid his hand from her shoulder up to her neck, urging her closer. He brought his head down and pressed his lips to hers. He hoped the kiss would be reassuring, letting her know she wasn't alone in the world.

A pounding on the windows of the car made him jerk back so suddenly he hit his head on the visor. He was out of the car so fast Charli barely had time to blink.

'Dad, Dad, guess what?' Owen was jumping up and down, full of excitement.

'Dad?' Trinity was looking at him, completely confused. Her gaze swung over as Charli climbed from the car and came to stand beside them.

'What is it, mate?' He picked the boy up and then turned to look at his mother's house, where he knew Rose would be standing at the door, making sure the kids had crossed the road safely. 'Thanks, Mum.' He waved and then headed inside, leaving Charli and Trinity to follow. 'What are you so excited about?'

'We won the soccer match.'

'I know, mate. I was there, remember.'

'Oh, yeah. Is Cam's leg hurt?'

'Yes. He's got a cast on and he said he wants all the soccer team to write their names on it.'

'Cool. That is super-wicked, Dad.'

Logan smiled at his son's expression as he took him into the kitchen and deposited him on a stool.

'And when we got home, do you know what Grandma did? She let us have chocolate ice cream with bananas and cream and topping and sprinkles.'

'Wow, now, that's what I call a treat. Was it nice?' Logan looked towards the door, surprised Trinity and Charli hadn't followed. What was keeping them?

'It was so yum. Can we have something special here, too, Dad? Grandma wouldn't let us have two of the banana things.'

'Why do you think she didn't?'

'Because we'd get sick?'

'Exactly. You don't want that, especially when I think we should go to Ararat for a special celebratory dinner tonight.'

'Wow! So many treats. This is *wick-ed*!' He slid off the stool. 'I'm going to tell Trin.' He ran off through the house, calling his sister's name. Moments later, Charli came into the kitchen, her expression concerned.

'Something wrong?'

'Trinity. She saw us kissing and then she told me to stay away from you.'

Logan groaned and shook his head. 'Where is she?'

'She ran off behind the house.'

'OK. I'll go talk to her.'

'You know where she is?'

'Yes. She has a favourite hiding spot, has done ever since she was little.' He headed out of the kitchen, only to be accosted by Owen.

'Dad, where's Trin?'

'She's outside. Leave her for the moment, Owen. Why don't you tell Charli about the surprise?' Logan met Charli's gaze over his son's head and conveyed the unspoken message that he needed her to keep Owen occupied. Charli nodded.

'Tell me all about it,' she said, holding out her hand to the five-year-old, who went willingly with her. Logan walked to the back yard, continuing down to the far right corner of the garden where a large weeping willow hung, its branches making a circular curtain, providing a private place inside them.

Logan paused just outside the canopy. 'Trin?'

'Go away.'

He stepped through and his heart constricted when he saw her sitting at the base of the trunk, her knees pulled up tight against her chest, her arms hugging them close. She looked up at him, her face tearstained.

'Oh, sweetheart.' He wanted to gather her to him, just as he had for the last five years every time something or someone had hurt her. At the same time, he also knew he needed to respect her privacy. Instead, he sat down next to her and stretched his legs out in front of him, crossing them at the ankles. He stayed silent, waiting for her to talk.

'You *kissed* her.' The words tumbled out and she tried to edge away from him.

'Yes.'

'Are you going to marry her?'

Logan exhaled sharply, knowing she needed answers but not sure he could give her any. 'I honestly don't know, Trin.'

'Are you going to leave me? Leave me and Owen?' A fresh bout of tears accompanied her words and Logan felt his own eyes fill with tears.

'Oh, Trin.' Unable to resist any longer, he dragged her into his arms and held her tight. 'Of course I'm not going to leave you—or Owen. You're my kids. You're my family. You mean *everything* to me, sweetheart. I love you.'

'But we're not your real kids. If you get married, things will change and you might have some more kids and then there'll be no room for me and Owen.'

Logan took a breath. He might not know the answers to some of her questions but he knew the answers to these ones. 'You and Owen are as real to me as if you *were* my own. You're both my family, my flesh and blood. I'm not going anywhere, Trin, and if things begin to change in our life, then we'll talk about it. We're a family and we do things together, and that includes Grandma and Grandad.'

'But you were kissing Charli.'

'Yes.' Logan brushed away her tears. 'Yes, I was.'

'So do you love her?'

Logan thought about that question. Did he? 'I don't know. I *like* her and I'd like her to stay for a while so we can all get to know her better, but I don't think she can.'

'Why not?'

'Because this isn't her home, sweetheart.' Logan tightened his arms around his girl. 'Charli lives in another country, in America. She has a home, a job, and her mother's there.'

'But she can't remember any of that, can she?'

'She's starting to remember more and more each day.'

'So, when she remembers, she'll go back?'

'She might need to go back so she *can* remember.' He thought of the best way to explain it. 'Charli has what the doctors call hysterical amnesia. Something has happened to her which has made her brain block out her memories. Being here in Halls Gap, nothing is familiar to her because she's never been here before, but if she goes back to her home and sees her mother again, maybe she'll remember.'

'So she's going to go away? Even though we like her?'

'Yes, princess.' He kissed the top of her head. 'She needs to go. Once Wil gets in contact with her mother, things should move pretty quickly.'

Trinity pulled back a little and looked at him. 'Are you going to kiss her again?' The look of disgust on her face made Logan laugh.

'Probably. If she lets me.'

'Do you *like* kissing her? It looks yuck.'

He laughed again as he stood, holding her tightly in his arms. 'You might not think so when you get older.'

'I'm *never* going to kiss a boy,' she declared. 'Except for you and Owen and Grandad. That's all.'

'Can I get that in writing?' Logan carried her back into the house. 'Let's go find Charli and Owen because I know she was very worried about you.'

They found them in Owen's room, sitting at the computer. 'This is how you jump up and down and this button helps to make you go faster and then you get more points.' Owen was giving Charli instructions on how to play the mathematical pirate game he loved so much.

Charli turned when she saw them and Owen did, too. He paused the game and faced his sister. 'Guess what? We're going out to dinner tonight in Ararat.'

'Cool.'

Charli's gaze met Logan's and he smiled, watching as she visibly relaxed. Trinity walked over to her.

'I'm sorry I yelled at you.'

Charli was surprised but smiled. 'That's OK. I'm sorry if I upset you.'

'Dad told me he likes kissing you so he'll probably do it again, but that's OK, even though I think kissing is gross.'

Logan looked away and cleared his throat before raising his gaze to meet Charli's once more. His smile was sheepish and he noticed Charli was slightly embarrassed at Trinity's forwardness.

'Look at this, Trin. I'm through to the next level. I can do this all by myself.' It was Owen who broke the awkward moment and Logan was able to remember to drag air into his lungs.

'Five more minutes, mate, and then we need to get ready to go out and celebrate.'

'Yahoo!' both kids said, but their faces were glued to the computer screen. Logan turned and walked out of the room, unable to believe Trinity had said what she had. A minute or two later Charli joined him in the kitchen, where he was waiting for the kettle to boil.

'Coffee?' he asked.

Charli nodded. 'I think we both need one.' She smiled shyly

at him and came around the bench to stand in front of him.
'So…you like kissing me, then?'

Logan leaned back against the cupboards and crossed his
legs at the ankles. 'Wasn't it obvious?' He folded his arms
across his chest, trying to block out the surge of awareness
coursing through him.

Charli began to feel that now familiar pounding in her chest
as she edged a little closer to him. Her tongue came out to
wet her lips and she watched as Logan's eyes darkened as his
gaze took in the action.

'You know, I'm not sure I can…remember.' She raised her
eyebrows suggestively and placed her hands on his arms. They
unfolded instantly and he dragged her closer. 'Maybe you'd
better…um…refresh my memory.'

'With pleasure.' Logan enveloped her in his arms and
brought his mouth down to meet hers. This time the sensations
were full of reciprocated pleasure and familiarity, which instantly set him ablaze.

Her fingers came up, threading through his hair, lightly massaging his scalp, and Logan groaned. She was becoming far
too important, far too addictive. His peace of mind was being
threatened…and he loved it!

Never had a woman been so direct with him, so giving and
inviting. The way their lips met, the way they instinctively
knew what the other needed, the way they seemed so in tune
with each other. He was going under—way under—and it
wasn't as frightening as he'd once thought it might be.

She broke away, gasping for air, but continued her assault
on his senses. Light, nibbling kisses were spread along his jaw,
around his neck and up to his ear. He shuddered as her teeth
nipped lightly at his earlobe, stirring every primal instinct in
him to life.

The kettle, the coffee, the kids—everything was forgotten.
There was only the two of them, in their own universe, and
nothing else mattered. Unable to take her nibbling torture any
longer, he shifted his head so their lips could meet once
more—both of them impatient for the way they made each
other feel.

Finally, they broke apart, their breathing intense as they held each other tight.

'Hmm.' Charli leaned her head against his chest. 'That's what I remember.'

'Does that mean you're cured?'

'Oh, no.' She pulled back to look at him. 'Far from it.'

A small smile spread across Logan's face. 'Glad to hear it.' He heard footsteps coming down the corridor and reluctantly let her go. Moments later Trinity came into the room.

'When are we leaving, Dad? Can I watch the *Nutcracker*?'

'The *Nutcracker*?' Charli looked at Trinity. 'Do you like that ballet?'

'Yes. I have it on video. Well, it's a cartoon one, not with real people. Do you like it, too?'

Charli smiled. 'It's my favourite.'

'Clara is the best,' Trinity said, climbing onto a stool. 'She is so brave but she's scared at the beginning but then she believes in herself and then she is the sugar plum princess who can do anything.'

Charli gasped, the smile slipping from her face as Trinity talked.

'What's wrong, Charli?'

'Nothing,' Logan answered for her. 'Sorry, Trin. You don't have time to watch TV now. We'll be going soon but perhaps you and Charli can watch it tomorrow.'

'Can we, Charli?'

Charli looked at the bright eyes of the child before her. 'I'd love to. Tchaikovsky is my favourite composer.'

'Who?'

'He's the man who wrote the music for the ballet,' Logan explained. 'Go and get ready and tell Owen to close down the computer.'

Trinity gave a whoop of delight and raced off, calling to her brother as she went.

'Believe in yourself. Well, at least that's one mystery solved.'

'One down, a few thousand to go.' She chuckled and smiled at him.

'I'm sorry we don't have time for that cup of coffee.'

'That's all right. I didn't mind its replacement.' She smiled at him, wanting nothing more than for him to repeat the kisses they'd shared before Trinity had interrupted them.

'Don't look at me like that,' he warned. 'We have to get going.' Logan stood, his gaze still flicking between her eyes and her lips.

Charli laughed, amazed at the surge of empowerment that coursed through her veins. What was it about this man which made her feel so free? She felt giddy with excitement but she wasn't quite sure what she was excited about.

'Go!' She laughed at him. 'Or we'll never get out of here.'

'OK.' He smiled and headed out of the kitchen, calling to his children as he went. Charli hugged herself, feeling a happiness she knew to be pure. Logan liked to kiss her! She liked to kiss him! Surely this was good—wasn't it?

Logical thoughts began to intrude on her euphoria and she instantly pushed them away. She didn't want to be sensible, she didn't want to be in control. She wanted to be reckless, to live in the moment, to listen to her heart and do the things she wanted to do. She wanted to believe in herself!

The necklace from Chuck—whoever he was—was in a drawer by the bed. She hadn't felt right wearing it, especially when all she'd wanted to do was to kiss Logan. Her smile increased again and she sighed, recalling how wonderful it felt to have his lips pressed firmly against hers. She knew she had a life back in America and she knew she might be setting not only herself but Logan up for future hurt, but she was following her instincts and believing in herself.

What about Logan? The question popped into her head and she opened her eyes, the euphoric feeling disappearing. Was she important to him? Was she just another person on his long list of people to help? She knew he couldn't help but give, it was who he was, but what happened when she no longer needed him any more? What would happen when she finally recovered her memory, which, as she was remembering more and more, was almost a certainty. Would Logan need her then?

Would he move on to someone else who needed him more? Was he attracted to her because of her vulnerability?

Questions. Too many questions. Charli sat down at the table and rested her head in her hands, closing her eyes tightly.

A flash appeared and she once more saw the Monet painting. This time she was able to recognise the room. It was in an office, *her* office. No. She couldn't see a desk. She saw a lab bench and testing equipment and realised it was a research lab.

'Charli?'

She opened her eyes to find Owen standing beside her.

'Come on! It's time to go. Dad says to get a coat because it will turn cold later, and he said that before we go to dinner we get to go to the flower show that's there. It's going to be boring and I'd rather go to the park but Dad says you haven't seen the flowers so we should go and look at the flowers, but come *on*, Charli.' Owen had taken her hand in his during his speech and was all but tugging her out of the room. 'Get a coat. Dad's ready to get in the car.'

'OK.' She smiled down at him. 'Come and help me find a coat.'

'Just put any one on. Come on,' he said impatiently.

'Don't listen to him,' Trinity said. 'I'll help you choose a coat.' Trinity took custody of the hand Owen had been tugging on. 'Owen, leave her alone and go and get in the car. Come on, Charli.'

Charli found herself tugged along by Logan's other child, into the room she was staying in. Trinity threw open the cupboard and looked at its contents. 'Nope.' She headed over to one of the boxes and opened the lid. She looked through. 'Not that one.' She pointed to the box below. 'Can you get this one for me, please?'

'Sure.' Charli was too flabbergasted at the request to do anything other than obey. She moved the top box off and Trinity opened the one below. 'This is it.' She pulled out a few clothes and then held up a warm coat. 'I have a photo of my mum wearing this coat and I think it's pretty. I'm keeping it for when I can wear it, but you can wear it tonight if you like.'

Charli was touched and met the girl's gaze. 'Thank you. I'd love to wear it.'

'There's also a nice skirt hanging up here and that light blue top goes really nicely with it.'

Charli looked at Trinity in surprise. 'Do you like clothes?'

'Yes, and shoes. My grandma does, too, and sometimes we go shopping together and that's so much fun. Grandma says that Dad just doesn't understand the shopping thing.' Trinity pointed to the skirt and top, eager for Charli to remove them from the hanging rail. 'Sometimes I come in here and look at the clothes and sometimes I try them on, although I can only do that when Grandma's here. I had this skirt and this top on the other week so Grandma's washed and ironed them because I spilt my drink on them and got upset, but Grandma wasn't even cross!'

Charli had taken the clothes down and removed them from the hangers.

'Go on,' Trinity urged. 'They look really good with the coat, too.'

Making sure the door was closed, Charli slipped out of her clothes and pulled the skirt and top on. The skirt came to just above her knee, revealing her legs, and was made of a soft, feminine fabric. The fact that the skirt felt foreign against her skin made her wonder if she'd ever had time for frivolous shopping in the past or whether the business suit she'd been pictured in at Logan's medical conference was all she ever wore.

'It's a twirly skirt,' Trinity said, sighing in envy. Charli laughed and obliged with a twirl. She looked at herself in the mirror and realised the blue top brought out the colour of her eyes. Pulling the band from her hair, she shook her head, the blonde strands falling around her face and shoulders.

'You're so beautiful, Charli. I want to be beautiful like you when I grow up.'

Charli smiled at her. 'You're beautiful now.' She did another twirl. 'Think this will do?'

'Yes. Now put the coat on. Oh…shoes.' Trinity ducked into the cupboard again and pulled out a pair of strappy sandals. 'These are my favourite.'

'Then I'll wear them,' Charli instantly responded, and slipped her feet into the two-inch heels.

'Make-up. You need make-up.' Another search revealed make-up and after Charli had applied some mascara and lipstick to herself, she put some on Trinity as well.

'Grandma doesn't let me wear make-up. She says I'm too young.'

'Well, tonight's a special occasion. Besides, I'm sure your dad won't mind.' Charli ran her fingers through the girl's long brown curls. 'Your hair is so gorgeous. Mine hardly ever curls.'

'I like yours.' Trinity giggled. 'We can both wear our hair down and be the same tonight, but first I need to put on a skirt, too.' She raced out of the room and came back quickly with two different skirts. 'Which one do you think?'

Charli smiled brightly at the way they were doing the full-on 'girly' thing. 'The red one.'

Trinity held it against herself and then nodded in agreement. 'Yes. You're right. I have shoes that go perfectly with it.' She slipped out of her pants and pulled the skirt on. 'I'll just get my shoes— Oh, and what about jewellery?'

'Trin?' Logan's voice sounded through the house. 'What are you girls doing?'

Charli giggled. 'I think the jewellery will have to wait for another time. The boys seem impatient to go.'

'Yeah, they always are. I'll get my shoes.' She raced off again and Charli stood, smoothing her hand down the foreign clothes. She looked at her reflection again, amazed at how happy she looked.

'Wow!' Logan stood in the open doorway and literally gaped. Charli turned and smiled when she saw him. She did a little twirl, showing off her new outfit.

'You look…' He swallowed, unable to finish his sentence. He didn't need to as she read the answer in his darkening gaze.

She cleared her throat. 'Trinity's letting me borrow them

for tonight.' His daughter came back into the room, her shoes on her feet, and crossed to Charli's side.

'What do you think, Dad? Don't we look beautiful?'

'Uh…' Logan swallowed again, looking from one to the other. Trinity had her arms around Charli's waist, smiling brightly. 'Yes.' He nodded. 'You both look…breathtaking.'

Trinity beamed at her father. He knew his children were coming to enjoy having Charli around as much as he was, and he sincerely hoped he wasn't setting them all up for a huge fall when she left…as he knew she must. The need to keep Charli with him strengthened once more.

Get a grip, Logan. Your daughter is in the room, your son is the car waiting for you, and all you can think about is kissing Charli senseless. He closed his eyes for a moment and then looked at his daughter again. 'Are you wearing make-up?'

'Charli put it on.' She tugged at Charli's hand. 'Come on. Let's go.'

Charli allowed herself to be led out to the car, conscious that Logan's gaze devoured her with every step she took—not that she minded! Her smile was one of feminine satisfaction, knowing she had the power to affect him so completely.

They all piled into the car and Logan reversed out of the driveway. She felt happy…and it was nice. What was it about this man *and* these children? Both children kept up a constant excited chatter on the drive, but the closer they got to Ararat, the more Charli felt her mood change and her heart begin to constrict with fear.

She glanced at her surroundings as Logan drove, taking in the scenery. When Logan reached over and touched her hand, she jumped, sucking in a breath. She coughed and cleared her throat, covering over her nervousness with a laugh, but when her gaze met his, she knew he'd seen something was wrong. Thankfully, he didn't say a word until he'd parked the car and the children were out.

'You can have ten minutes to play in the park,' he told them as he pointed over the grassy knoll to the play equipment.

'Awesome, Dad!' Owen said, and he and Trinity raced off.

Logan watched them and, without looking at her, he took Charli's hand in his and started walking slowly towards the park.

'What have you remembered?' His voice was quiet yet Charli heard the concern in it.

'I remember driving through here...' She indicated the main street in Ararat. 'It was dark, the streets were deserted, but I remember it. I remember the drive into Halls Gap. Coming along that same road just now, it all came flooding back.'

Logan nodded. As she spoke, he could feel her begin to shake. 'Perhaps we should go for a walk to where we found you near the Venus Baths.'

'That's...logical.' Her tone was sceptical.

'But?'

'But I don't know if I can.' She stopped walking and turned to face him. 'Honestly, Logan, just coming here, my chest feels constricted as though it's going to implode. My hands are perspiring, my thoughts are all jumbled.'

Logan didn't need her to tell him anything. The fear she felt was there in her eyes, which were gazing at him with hope...hope that she wouldn't have to face her thoughts alone. Without a word, he pulled her into his arms and held her tight.

'It's going to be OK. I'm here to help you.'

Reluctantly, Charli pulled back and looked at him. 'I know you are, but there are going to be things only I can face, Logan. Things I *have* to face so I can unravel this puzzle that surrounds me. I know I need to do this, but at the same time I don't know if I can.'

'You're a strong woman, Charli. That much I *do* know about you.' He rested his hands on her shoulders and looked down into her beautiful face. 'You will get through this, get your memory back, and use the whole experience to your advantage.'

'You think so?'

'I know so. Now, how about we go and look at some flowers before having that celebratory dinner?'

'Yes. I need to let my mind relax for a while.'

Logan called to his children and, not letting go of Charli's hand, they all walked over to the flower display. Sometimes Owen held Charli's other hand, sometimes Trinity did. All four of them seemed quite content, and once they'd walked around the grounds they headed across the road to the restaurant, where he watched as Charli continued to laugh and enjoy herself.

Once they'd finished dessert, Logan ordered himself and Charli a coffee. Both of the children had gone to another table to talk to some of their school friends and to tell them about the soccer game. Logan could feel the interested looks he knew they were receiving on account of Charli joining their family party.

'You know we're the main topic of discussion tonight, don't you?' he murmured to Charli as they waited for their coffees.

'Does that bother you?'

'No.'

'You don't mind that people have connected us romantically?'

Logan smiled and shrugged. 'Wouldn't they be right?'

Charli returned his smile and sat back in her chair as the waitress put the coffee cups on the table.

'Thank you, Bernice.' Logan smiled at the waitress who Charli guessed to be in her early twenties. Bernice flushed slightly under Logan's smile and lowered her eyes for a moment before leaving them alone.

Charli shook her head at Logan. 'Do you have any idea how lethal your smiles are, Dr Hargraves?'

'Pardon?'

Charli smiled and shook her head again. 'Typical. That poor girl was almost knocked off her feet just because you smiled at her.'

'Oh. Really?' Logan glanced over his shoulder at Bernice who was watching them and quickly looked away.

'You seem surprised.' Charli laughed a little. 'Don't have a clue how you affect women, do you,' she stated rhetorically.

'I doubt it's just me. I'm sure Bernice would blush and go all coy if any man smiled at her. It's just the age she is.'

Charli laughed again. 'Careful, Logan. You're starting to sound like an old man.'

'Well, I'm far too old for her at any rate.' He picked up his coffee and took a sip, the napkin sticking to the bottom of the cup. 'Spilt again. Why do they do this?' he asked as he pulled the napkin off. 'Why do they put it under the cup? It isn't going to do me any good if I want to wipe my mouth because it's already soaked up with the coffee she spilt carrying it over.'

Charli's eyes sparkled with delight at his tirade. She picked up her own cup and had the same thing happen. They both laughed. Logan reached over and pulled her napkin off, then frowned as another piece of paper appeared to be stuck to the bottom of her cup. 'Hold on.' He peeled it off and opened it.

The laughter disappeared from his face and he quickly glanced around the restaurant.

'We're leaving.'

'Logan?' Charli felt a prickle of apprehension wash over her. 'Logan? What is it?'

Logan held the note firmly in his hand. 'Don't worry about it.' He called to his children.

'Logan? Let me see.'

'You don't want to.'

'Logan!' Charli was now starting to get very worried.

Logan glanced down at the paper in his hand before reluctantly giving it to her. Charli opened it with trembling fingers and read the smudged words.

Charlotte, I've found you.

CHAPTER EIGHT

CHARLI was still trembling when Logan helped her through the front door of his house and removed her coat. Thankfully, the children had kept up a steady chatter on the drive back, accompanied by many yawns, and now Logan was telling them to brush their teeth and to start getting ready for bed.

'Stay here,' he told Charli as he led her to a seat in the living room. 'I won't be long.' Logan knelt down beside her as she sat, reaching his hand out to tenderly tuck a few strands of hair behind her ears. 'You'll be fine.' He stood and brushed his lips reassuringly against hers before turning and walking out of the room.

She heard him rushing his kids through their night-time routine, and although she felt sorry that she was the cause of his impatience, she was also grateful that the sooner they were settled in bed, the sooner Logan would be back at her side.

Fifteen minutes later, he came back into the living room and sat down beside her. He reached out and took her hand in his. 'Charli?' Her name sounded like a caress and she turned to face him. Logan clenched his jaw when he saw the unshed tears glistening in her eyes.

'I'm so scared, Logan,' she whispered, her lower lip beginning to crumple. 'Someone is looking for me and it's petrifying.'

'Do you know who?'

She shook her head. 'But now I know why I didn't want to stay in hospital, why I haven't wanted to be left alone.'

He nodded. 'I was thinking about that, too. If someone was looking for you, then checking the hospitals would be an obvious first step.' He squeezed her hand. 'You're safe here.'

'Am I? I don't think so. Not any more. Don't you see, the person who wants to find me *saw* me with you tonight. All he had to do was to follow us home. He could be out there, right now! I've put you in danger, not to mention your children.' Her voice cracked on the last few words and the tears which had been threatening to fall ever since she'd read the note started to slide down her cheeks.

'Hey. Shh.' Logan touched her face, smoothing her hair back. 'We'll work it out—*together*.'

'I can't bring you into this.'

'We're already there, Charli.'

'Don't say that. That's more guilt to lay at my door should anything happen to you.' She wrenched free from him and stood, starting to pace. 'I need to move, I need to walk.' She headed for the door.

Logan was out of his chair like a shot. 'No!' He grabbed her shoulders and pointed her in the direction of the corridor. 'You can't go outside. Pace up and down here.'

'But I'll wake the children.'

Logan shrugged. 'Walk quietly. Besides, I'd rather you wake the kids than have something else happen to you.' He pulled his cellphone from his jeans and punched in a number.

'Who are you calling?'

'Wil.'

'What can he do about it?'

'I don't know. Analyse the handwriting, check out this house to make sure no one's waiting outside. Make enquiries at the restaurant we were at tonight.'

'But you've already done that,' Charli protested, but Logan wasn't listening. He was describing the situation to Wil.

'Yeah, I asked the waitress, Bernice was her name, if she'd seen or spoken to anyone,' he told Wil. 'She said she had and gave a description of a man who had come to the bar when she was making our coffees at the counter. She said he had a nice smile, blond hair and grey eyes. She said he'd chatted for a few minutes but hadn't ordered any food or drinks. She was pretty shaken up when I told her this man may have put a note beneath Charli's cup.'

'Did he have an accent? Was he American?'

'She didn't say and I didn't ask. Questioning is your field

of expertise, not mine. I just wanted to get Charli and the kids
out of there as soon as possible.'

'Have you spoken to the Ararat police about this?'

'No.'

'OK. I'll get onto it. Now, give me specifics. What time did
you arrive at the restaurant? Where did you go before that?'

Charli continued to pace up and down the corridor while
Logan talked. The more she walked, the easier it was to think.
Her emotions began to change from fear to anger. Strength
began to build up and she knew that whatever it was or—
more to the point—*whoever* it was who was looking for her
wouldn't go away, so she may as well face it. And she'd be
glad to…if she could remember! She growled with frustration,
her pace increasing.

'OK. I'd better go. Charli's about to wear a hole through
my floorboards.'

'You don't have floorboards,' Wil pointed out. 'You have
a cement slab.'

'Either way, she'll do structural damage to my home if I let
her go any longer. Call me when you have something.' Logan
rang off and Charli gave him a withering look.

'What was all that supposed to mean?' She spun on her heel
to face him.

'Charli.' Logan headed up the corridor and took her hand
in his. She wrenched away.

'Don't touch me.'

'Hey! I'm not the bad guy here,' Logan said, but didn't
make any further move to touch her. 'Come into the kitchen
where we can talk, and I'll make you a drink.'

'I don't want a drink.'

'Come on. There's even room to pace. Maybe not as long
as the corridor here but, still, room to move. Tea or coffee…or
something a little stronger?' When he received no reply, he
turned and left her to it, switching on the kettle. A moment or
two later, Charli stormed right over to him and stood toe to
toe with him.

'Don't tell me what to do. Got it?'

'Got it.'

'And don't tell me everything's going to be all right, because it isn't.'

'OK.'

'I'm mad.'

'I can see that.'

'I'm livid, furious, incensed beyond belief.'

'I believe you.'

'How *dare* someone make me feel this way? It's so unfair, especially when I can't remember anything.'

Logan nodded, unsure what he was supposed to say.

'I'm trying so hard to remember, Logan, *so hard*, but it doesn't work like that, and then out of the blue—whoosh—I'm flooded with memories. That number, that big number I remembered, is for the safe in my laboratory. It's on the wall, behind a Monet painting.' She spread her arms wide. 'I don't even know where my laboratory is!'

'Wil can find—'

'Wil can find out, yes, I know, but why can't my brain just click back into place and start working normally again? I'm starting to remember things but only every now and then. It's like…Swiss cheese. Lots of holes in it.'

Logan nodded. 'That's the way it is, sweetheart. I wish I could snap my fingers and make it all better, but I can't.' He raked a hand through his hair, his own frustration building. 'We have got to do everything we can to remain focused about this, even when it drives us insane.'

'I know you're right.' Charli was amazed to feel her anger beginning to fade. 'But it's highly annoying.'

'That's one word for it. I can think of a few more, such as harassment, badgering and emotional manipulation. We need to get to the bottom of this, Charli, and *that* I promise you, we will do.'

She walked over to him and wrapped her arms about his waist. Logan instantly embraced her, holding her close. 'You have no idea what it means to me to know I'm not alone in this.'

'I can guess.'

'I don't want to go back to America,' she mumbled.

'I know.'

'When the time comes…' She stopped, hesitated and then pulled back slightly to look at him. 'When the time comes, will you come with me?'

Logan looked down into her blue eyes and the anguish he saw there twisted his gut. 'I don't think I can.'

Charli nodded sadly and he felt awful for letting her down. 'I have responsibilities here and they're not that easy to get out of. I have my children, my clinic, the hospital.'

'Yeah. Yeah. I know.' She shrugged and stepped back from his embrace. 'No harm in asking, though.' Her words were spoken softly and he could hear the hurt in her tone. She wasn't trying to manipulate him…not on purpose…but it was working nevertheless.

'Charli.' He reached for her but she shook her head and he raked a hand through his hair.

'I need to try and sleep.'

'Are you going to be able to?'

'I hope so. I need to have my wits about me if I'm going to beat this guy.'

'Chuck?'

She raised her gaze to his and nodded. 'Yes. It's Chuck. I feel it.'

'And the necklace?'

She shook her head. 'I don't know. If he's…romantically connected with me, it's well and truly over, especially as he's scaring me stupid.'

Logan nodded. 'Believe in yourself.'

The tension drained out of Charli and she dragged in a cleansing breath. 'Yes. Yes.'

'I'll double-check all the locks on the doors,' Logan said softly. 'Let me know if you want any paracetamol or even a sleeping tablet. There's nothing wrong with taking one in this instance.'

'I'll be fine.' She headed out of the room but stopped as Logan's cellphone rang.

'It's Wil,' he said, reading the name on the LCD screen, and quickly connected the call. 'What's the news?'

'I've patrolled past your house and there are no suspicious cars in the neighbourhood.'

'Good to hear.'

'Ararat police have spoken to Bernice and they're getting an artist to draw up a picture from her description. She said he had a...different accent, but she wasn't sure from where.'

'It's a start.'

'Apparently she said he had hypnotic grey eyes and a nice smile. Why can't girls say that about me?'

Logan smiled a little, glad Wil had eased the tension a little. 'Gee, mate. I have no idea.'

'How's Charli holding up?'

Logan's gaze met Charli's. 'She's not doing too badly, given the circumstances. Probably coping better than you or I would.'

'Now, that's saying something. OK, buddy. Stay safe and I'll check back with you if I find out anything more.'

'I'd appreciate it.' Logan rang off and passed the information on to Charli about the artist and that the man had an accent.

Charli closed her eyes and rubbed her fingers over her forehead. 'I think I'll take that paracetamol now, if that's all right.'

Logan opened the cupboard door. 'That's more than all right.' He handed the tablets to her, watched her swallow them, and then they walked down the corridor towards the bedrooms. He checked both of his children and was surprised when Charli followed him into their rooms. She didn't say a word until they were standing outside her bedroom door.

'I'm sorry, Logan.'

'What for?'

'For dragging you into this mess.'

'You didn't drag me and we still don't know what sort of mess it is.' He gathered her into his arms and pressed his lips to hers. 'I'm sure, whatever it is, you'll meet it head on and triumph.'

'How do you know?'

'Because the good guys are supposed to finish first.'

'Am I a good guy, though?' The question was asked very softly but Logan had to admit she had a point.

'I know it sounds clichéd but, whatever happens, you'll do the right thing.'

'How do you know?'

'Because you have an honest heart. Regardless of the fact that you can't remember who you are or who's after you, you're honest, Charli, and you need to hold firm to that. Trust your instincts, just as you've been doing, and you won't go wrong.'

'My instincts are telling me that I don't want to be alone tonight.'

Logan dragged in a deep breath and looked down into her beautiful face. 'That's understandable.'

'Can I sleep in your room?'

Logan swallowed. 'Charli, I—'

'Just hold me, Logan. I need to feel safe. I see the way you do it with your kids and I envy them. You hold them in your arms, as though you're never going to let go, and the look on their faces is one of pure trust and security. I need that tonight, Logan.'

Logan pressed his lips to hers before letting her go and taking a big step backwards. He exhaled harshly and raked his hand through his hair. 'I don't know if I can, Charli. Sleep in my bed, by all means, but I don't think I can be there.'

Charli saw the desire in his eyes and her heart immediately began to tattoo that wild, uncontrollable rhythm which happened whenever he looked at her this way. 'You don't think we can control ourselves?'

'We can try, but it's too risky. You must see that. Taking…whatever it is between us any further won't do either of us any favours in the long run.'

'You're right.' Charli sighed and shook her head. 'I'm sorry.'

'No,' he implored. 'Don't be sorry. *Please*, don't be sorry.' He gathered her close into his arms again and pressed his lips to hers. He kissed her with renewed passion, wanting to acknowledge what was between them but knowing if he didn't keep control over what he was feeling for her, then regardless of the measures he'd put in place to protect his heart, they wouldn't do any good. She was amazing, delightful, invigorating and highly addictive. He moved his mouth over hers with a slow deliberation he knew was wrong, but he was unable to resist. This much, at least, he was allowing himself, and from the way she was responding it was clear they were on the same wavelength.

'Daddy!'

The sound of his son calling out into the night had him freezing and then slowly drawing away from the enchanting woman before him.

'Daddy!' The call came again and Logan stepped reluctantly away. 'I'd better go see to him before he wakes Trin up.'

Charli nodded and stepped back into her bedroom.

'Honestly, Charli, if you want to sleep in my room, please, feel free. After all, it's not as though I'm going to get much sleep tonight.'

Charli grimaced at his words. 'You and me both—but I have to at least try.' She smiled at him. 'I'll be fine in here.'

'OK. Besides, in a few more hours—well, about eight more—you'll probably have both of my children climbing into bed with you.'

'Envious?' She smiled at the way he groaned and rolled his eyes.

'What do you think?' Owen called out again and Logan took another step away. 'Try and sleep,' he said softly. 'See you in the morning.' With that, he forced his legs to take him in the other direction before he capitulated completely.

When Charli awoke on Sunday morning, it was to find the bedclothes completely tangled and only half covering her. She gently felt around in the bed but couldn't find anyone else there. No children. No Logan.

'It's for the best,' she mumbled to herself as she stood and stretched. She made her bed, found a change of clothes and tiptoed over to the bathroom. The rest of the house still appeared to be quiet and she wondered whether Logan had managed to get any sleep or not.

Her own dreams had been such a jumbled mixture, she felt exhausted. One minute she was being chased. She'd been driving in a gold car, speeding up so no one could catch her, and the next minute she was out on the soccer field, kicking a goal with Owen. Logan, dressed as a referee, clapped loudly and ran over to kiss her.

'Too many emotions,' she whispered beneath the shower spray. Once she was showered and dressed, she felt a little less like she'd been pulverised. She went in search of the children who were usually up at this time, but there was no sign of them. Their beds were made and she wondered if anyone in this house had slept last night. Were they in bed with Logan? She glanced up the hallway to his door and instantly her heart rate increased.

Shaking her head, she went into the kitchen and there she saw a note on the bench. 'Just getting breakfast. Won't be long.' She read it out loud and smiled at the way Trinity had written it, signing all their names at the bottom.

It wasn't long before they returned with delicious croissants and rolls from the bakery.

'Did you sleep all right?' Logan asked while he made them coffee.

'Not really.' Charli shrugged nonchalantly. 'But I know there's nothing I could do about it.'

Logan didn't say anything else, nodding instead. 'All right, kids. Let's get breakfast under way because, when we've finished, we'll be taking Charli for a walk to the Venus Baths.'

'Aw, *wick-ed*,' Owen said. 'That's my favourite place.'

Logan watched Charli closely and saw the fear and uncertainty in her eyes. He was glad she wasn't facing this alone, that he'd be there to help her through it. She picked at her food but he really didn't blame her for not having much of an appetite when her mind was probably whirring almost out of control with the possible scenarios she might unlock.

Once they were done, she loaded the dishwasher and turned

it on. The kids already had their jackets on and were waiting outside.

'Come on.' Logan's tone was quiet as he held her coat for her. 'No more stalling.'

'Who says I'm stalling?' she snapped.

'You may not remember anything, Charli,' he pointed out. She slipped her arms into the coat and then turned to lean her head against his chest. It was as natural as the sun shining that Logan should put his arms about her to hold her close.

'I know I will and I know I'm not going to like it.'

'Then the sooner we face it the better.' Logan pulled back and took her hand firmly in his. 'Come on. I'll be with you every step of the way.' Charli couldn't move. Logan bent his head and kissed her. 'It's time.'

'You'd planned to take me out to the Venus Baths all along,' she stated, and he nodded.

'You and I both know retracing your steps may help jog the memories.'

'You were waiting until I was in a better mental state to deal with it?'

'I was waiting until you were a little more sure of yourself.'

'You think I am? I don't.'

He smiled at her words.

'Don't laugh at me, Logan!'

'I'm not laughing *at* you, Charli. I would never do that.'

'I know. I'm just...'

'Anxious,' he supplied.

'Terrified,' she corrected.

He squeezed her hand. 'Come on.' Once he got her legs moving, leading her out of the kitchen and then out of the house, she seemed to settle down. They crossed the road and headed towards the path which led to the Venus Baths.

Charli took a deep breath and slowly let it out. She looked up at Logan and nodded. 'Right. Let's do this.'

Logan watched as her earlier tension left her and she raised her chin in defiance. She'd gathered her wits and was now ready to face the world—or, in her case, her past.

The kids had run on ahead, knowing the area like the backs

of their hands, so Logan was able to focus on Charli. He held her hand as they walked down the path, going further into the dense foliage, walking slowly.

Charli felt the now familiar constriction of her heart as fear once more gripped her. She looked around at her surroundings and knew instinctively she'd been there before. She stopped walking, closed her eyes and gripped Logan's hand as though it were her lifeline.

Her eyes were shut so tight, Logan's heart went out to her. The pain she was going through, the anguish—if only he could prevent it he would, but he knew it was impossible. Her lips parted to allow air to escape, and if he'd placed a stethoscope to her heart right now, he knew it would be pounding furiously in fear.

'Logan?' she whispered.

'I'm here.'

'I've been here.' She opened her eyes and took in her surroundings once more. 'I've walked along this path and I was…agitated.'

Logan urged her a little further until they came to a seat near a bridge. 'Sit down.' He pulled her close, hoping the body contact would help her to relax a little. 'Take a deep breath and let it out.'

She did as he'd suggested. 'I remember driving from Melbourne, through Ararat and then into the main road of Halls Gap. I stopped outside your clinic and noted the hours, then I drove and parked the car. It was still dark, well, almost time for dawn, and I needed to walk, to help get my thoughts in order. I got out of the car and headed in this direction. I had no idea where I was going but the tracks were signposted so I just followed them.'

'What were you so upset about?'

'That…' She sighed heavily. 'That I don't know.'

'Why did you stop outside the clinic?'

She turned and looked at him, his arm sliding off her shoulder and onto the back of the seat. 'I came here to see you.'

'To see *me*?' Logan couldn't have been more surprised if she'd whacked him over the head with a bit of two-by-four.

'But…' He frowned. 'We'd met for a brief instant, Charli. That was all.'

'I know.'

'You remember meeting me?'

She nodded. 'Yes.' She thought for another moment and nodded again. 'Yes. You shook my hand and smiled and…' She stopped and looked down.

'And?' Logan was astonished that he was so caught up in Charli's memories.

'And…I was mesmerised. I felt…something.'

'Ah. Yes.' He cleared his throat, feeling a touch uncomfortable but knowing they had to get through this. 'It was there, wasn't it? This…*thing* between us.'

'Yes. You told me you were from Halls Gap in the Grampians and I was so disappointed when you couldn't meet me for that drink.'

'You and me both! Do you remember giving your lecture? Anything else?'

She nodded. 'I remember searching the crowd for you while I was up on the podium. I had trouble concentrating.'

'Hmm. So did I.' He smiled at her. 'I think I wrote copious notes in that lecture because it was easier than looking up at you.'

'You seemed…enthralled with what I was saying.'

Logan nodded. 'I was enthralled by *you*—period.' This wasn't getting them anywhere. 'We need to focus now.'

'Yes.'

'So, after the lecture?'

'I went back up to my hotel room, kicked off my shoes and sat down to watch television. I was thinking of you, imagining us getting together for our drink.'

He groaned and closed his eyes for a moment. 'Focus,' he growled, more for his sake than hers. 'After that?' He was finding it more and more difficult not to haul her into his arms. This was part of her treatment and both of them needed to remain professional.

'I remember having breakfast on Monday morning in my room and then starting to tidy up. I tried calling my mother but received no reply. I was worried but I told myself it was probably coincidence.' Charli looked at him, fear in her eyes. 'Something is very wrong, Logan.'

'Yes.' He placed a kiss on her head. 'What else? Anything?'

'I tried to look over my notes but I couldn't concentrate properly.'

'Notes for what? The conference was finished by then.'

She thought hard. 'I...I can't remember.' Charli closed her eyes. 'After reading my notes, the next thing I can remember is...is driving through Ararat.'

'So you're missing a gap from after breakfast on Monday to early Tuesday morning.'

'All I know is that I had a need to go, to escape. I had to get away but I have no idea why. I got into the car and I just drove. I saw a sign that said "Grampians" and then I was going through Ararat.' She shrugged. 'The rest, I guess we know.'

'You came here to see me.' He was still stunned at the thought.

'Yes.'

'Why?'

'I...felt safe.'

Logan turned a little so he could look at her. 'Safe from what?'

'I don't know. I remember you saying you were from Halls Gap and I remember your eyes.'

'My eyes?'

'Yes. They were alive with life when you talked about your work here and I thought, Here is a man who likes what he does, who seems free and alive with the love of medicine.'

'You don't like what you do?'

'The more I think about it, the more I'm certain of it. I can't recall specifics but I'm not content with life the way you are. Perhaps that's why I need to believe in myself.'

'You don't like being a doctor, is that it?'

'I've loved helping you out since I arrived here so I'm not sure it's that.'

'Has this process we've gone through today helped you with any other memories?'

Charli thought for a moment and then sighed, feeling exhausted. 'I don't know, Logan. I'm starting to get a headache.'

'OK. Enough for today.' He hugged her close and kissed the top of her head. 'Why don't you stay here? I'll get the kids and then we can go and get an ice cream.'

Charli smiled up at him. 'Sounds nice.' Logan stood, placed a small kiss on her cheek and headed off down the path to get his children. Charli felt a lot of her earlier tension seep out, happy that what she'd remembered so far hadn't been too traumatic. She still had a sense of foreboding, knowing that it must have been something pretty bad to send her off into the state she was now in, but although there was still more to come, for now she was happy with the progress she'd made.

She glanced down the track in the direction Logan had disappeared, thankful he'd been with her. He really was becoming way too important in her life and she knew the feelings she'd been trying hard to fight since arriving here were now starting to get out of control. Logan meant a lot to her—as did his children. He wouldn't be the same person without Trinity and Owen, and she loved him for what he'd done for them and the sacrifices he'd made along the way.

Loved him?

She backed up to that thought and looked at it once more. Yes, he meant a lot to her, yes, she liked being with him, yes, she felt secure when his arms were around her—but surely that didn't mean she'd fallen in love with him, did it?

Charli groaned and buried her face in her hands as she acknowledged the truth of her feelings. Logan—both of the children—the town… The whole enchilada. During the short amount of time she'd spent here, she'd fallen in love with the place. The memory of those two squirming children beneath her bedcovers brought an instant smile to her face and she felt herself relax. And their father? Charli shook her head as though there was nothing she could do about it. She was one hundred per cent, prime time in love with him.

Her smile increased and she pulled her hands away from

her face. She loved Logan. She had no idea when it had sneaked up on her, but it was there right now, and even though she still had a long road ahead of her, regardless of what happened, he'd stolen her heart for ever.

'Charli!' Owen was calling her name and she turned to face him, her smile beaming as he ran directly up to her and grabbed her hand. 'We're going to get ice cream.' He tugged her up. 'Come on. Let's go.'

Trinity was hard on his heels and she grabbed for Charli's free hand. 'Ice cream, Charli. I'm going to have two different flavours.'

'I'm having peppermint and choc fudge,' Owen declared as they tugged her along. They all wouldn't fit down the path together and laughingly Charli let go of their hands.

'I'm having English toffee and pecan,' Trinity declared, falling into step behind her brother. Charli looked over her shoulder, wondering where Logan was, and as she turned, she felt him bump into her. The immediate contact produced zillions of little tingles throughout her body, making her gasp.

Her heart rate increased at the slight touch and her breath caught in her throat as Logan's arms came around her, making sure they didn't lose their balance.

'You OK?' He steadied her and then dropped his hands.

'Yea…' She cleared her throat. 'Yes. I'm fine.' She glanced up at him before turning and forcing her legs to move.

'You sure?'

'Yes.'

Neither of them spoke as they walked along the path. When it got to the stage where they could walk side by side, Logan quickly took her hand and Charli almost breathed a sigh of relief. She was astonished by the way he made her feel and couldn't believe she was behaving like a love-struck teenager.

'What flavour would you like?'

'Huh?' She turned wide eyes up to him, her breathing still not quite under control. He smiled and she felt herself sigh with longing. 'Uh…ice cream.' She licked her lips and noticed Logan's eyes darken a little, glad she wasn't the only one being affected here. 'Vanilla.'

'Vanilla?' Logan repeated incredulously. 'There's over thirty flavours to choose from and you choose vanilla?' He shook his head and tut-tutted. 'Charli, Charli, Charli. We're going to have to do something about that.'

She smiled up at him and laughed. 'Why? I like vanilla.'

Logan slung his arm about her shoulders, drawing her close. 'All right, then. Vanilla it is, but expect an outcry from the kids.' He looked over to where his children had reached the roadside, checked both ways and then turned to him for confirmation that it was all right for them to cross. 'Go on,' he called, and, after walking carefully across the road, they bolted into the ice-cream shop.

'They're so wonderful, Logan.' Charli stopped and looked at him. 'They really are such a credit to you.'

'And my parents,' he added.

'Just like you. Unable to take credit for it all when I'm sure you deserve most of it.' She reached up and brushed a lock of hair back from his forehead. She loved him. She loved this man. She still found it hard to believe and the elation of the discovery was now starting to take effect.

She couldn't think about her other life—the life she wasn't sure she wanted to unlock. Here, in Halls Gap, she was happy. She felt strong. Logan *helped* her to feel strong and he'd helped give that new-found strength wings. Charli felt as though she could soar like an eagle, that the world was her oyster, and that, with him by her side, anything was possible.

She believed in herself.

Was this how Clara had felt at the end of the *Nutcracker*? The ballet took on a whole new meaning for her and she couldn't wait to get back to Logan's house and enjoy watching it with Trinity.

He was looking at her now, his expression intense. She still wondered whether he would desire her as much once she'd regained her memories. Would he think she wouldn't need him then? If he did, he was wrong. She needed him now more than she'd ever needed anyone else—at least, that was the way she felt.

The overwhelming and encompassing feeling of love

swelled within her and choked off the words she wanted to say to him. She needed to show him, to show him how much he meant to her.

Her fingers went around to the back of his neck and she urged his head down, impatient for their lips to meet. When they were finally pressed together, Charli was swamped with the feeling of coming home. Regardless of what might happen as she slowly unlocked her memories, she knew this love was for ever and put everything she had into the kiss, wanting Logan to know how she felt.

She was a little surprised when he put his hands on her arms and gently pulled away. His eyes were glazed with desire but there was caution in his every breath. Charli wondered whether his feelings were as deep as hers and instantly put her guard up.

'Don't kiss me like that out here, Charli.' He glanced around at their surroundings. 'It's not fair…to either of us.'

She let out the breath she'd been unconsciously holding and gave him a little smile. 'For a moment there, I thought you didn't want to kiss me.'

'You're insane, then.' He took her hand and continued towards the road. 'Let's get some ice cream. Nice and…cold! Hopefully, that will sort us both out.'

Charli laughed as they walked across the road to the ice-cream shop. The kids had already chosen their flavours and were anxiously waiting for the treat to be handed over so they could eat it. Logan smiled as Charli declared she wanted vanilla and, as he'd predicted, protests came from both children. He caught sight of Wil's police car driving down the street and thought he'd better fill him in on Charli's recent breakthrough.

'Put it on the account, Mrs Blackwell,' he told the woman behind the counter. 'I'll be back in a moment,' he said to Charli. 'Just going to catch Wil.' He gave her hand a little squeeze before letting go and heading outside.

The kids went outside to sit in the small rotunda to eat their ice creams as Charli waited for hers. She'd just accepted her cone with thanks when she stepped back and bumped into someone. 'Oh, sorry,' she said, turning to apologise to the person. She looked directly into a pair of steel-grey eyes and her throat closed.

'Don't make any sudden moves.' The man nudged her with a small, black gun. His American accent penetrated her mind and she knew she knew him. 'Smile and don't let anyone know anything is wrong and you'll be fine. Go outside.' The fear she'd been intuitively feeling since her arrival here came surging up, clouding her thinking. 'I don't know why you bothered running from me, Charlotte.' He shook his head, his voice barely above a whisper. 'Not a good move.' He removed the ice cream from her hand and tossed it carelessly into a bin.

'Chuck!' The strangled word hardly made it past her throat as she walked with him.

He grinned at her, a smooth smile that would charm any woman—any woman who didn't know the true personality behind it. 'And here I'd heard you'd lost your memory. Looks as though you've done a good job of fooling everyone, honey, but not me.' He nudged her again. 'Let's go. The car's over there.'

Charli glanced over to where Trinity and Owen were sitting, eating their ice creams and waiting for her. Please, she prayed, don't let them look over. The thought that something might happen to them was paramount in her mind—which was slowly beginning to function again.

She looked towards the BMW convertible Chuck was steering her towards, his fierce grip on her arm hurting badly. She glanced around and it was then she saw Logan coming out of the police station with Wil beside him, both men laughing.

'Don't go getting any ideas, Charli. Lover-boy will be fine so long as you do as you're told.'

No sooner were the words out of Chuck's mouth than Logan looked over and saw her. She watched the confusion cross his face and then she dipped her head, her hair falling across her eyes, blocking out the sight of him.

'Almost there. You're doing just fine.'

'Charli? Where ya going?' The call came from behind her and she recognised Owen's voice.

'Don't do anything stupid.' Chuck's voice was gruff and held a thread of desperation. Charli wouldn't put it past him to do anything which he thought necessary to save his precious reputation. Flashes of memory were coming back to her in pieces but not enough to make a whole picture.

Chuck, touching the gold necklace around her throat.

Chuck, driving her out to a university where she was giving a lecture and telling her once more she would do as she was told.

Chuck, threatening to hurt her mother.

Chuck, chasing after her as she raced through the university to the gold hire car they'd driven in. She'd climbed frantically behind the wheel, fumbling with the keys she'd managed to snatch from his hand, desperate to get them into the ignition.

Chuck, picking up a rock and throwing it at the car as she drove away.

Charli tried to push the thoughts away. She needed to concentrate now. Her head was pounding but she worked through the pain. She needed to make sure that Logan and the children remained safe. It was the least she could do for the people she loved.

'Charli?' Now it was Logan who called out, and she glanced over to see him talking to Wil, his gaze firmly on her.

It happened as though in slow motion. She watched as Wil put his hand on his gun and unclipped it, although it remained in the holster, and started walking in their direction. He was talking to her, calling out to her and the man she was with, but Charli couldn't make out what he was saying. All she knew was that he was getting closer and she *had* to keep him away.

'No!' She yelled. 'Go back. He's got a gun!'

Logan froze where he was, his heart hammering with fear for Charli. He glanced over to where his kids were. Trinity was standing up, watching intently. Owen was starting to walk away from the rotunda.

He was on one side, the kids were on the other and Charli

was in the middle. Charli! *His* Charli. Logan's heart constricted and he had to remind himself to breathe, to keep a clear head. Mrs Blackwell came out of the shop and thankfully shepherded his kids back inside where they were safe.

One obstacle down.

Logan focused his attention on the woman who meant the world to him. What was going on? He squinted, looking closely at the man.

'Chuck!' The word was barely audible. Logan had seen him somewhere before and in an instant he recalled Chuck as the man who'd been speaking on his cellphone at the conference. Parts of the conversation Logan had overheard returned with clarity.

She'll play ball. I know her mother. I'll switch to more drastic measures. I'll take care of it.

Logan swallowed over the lump in his throat as the realisation hit—Charli's past had just caught up with her.

'Don't come any closer!' Chuck called, stopping both Logan and Wil in their tracks.

'Easy, mate.' Wil held up both hands. Logan wished for camouflage, for something to hide behind, but it was impossible. They were all exposed in the middle of the street and if it had been summer, the place would have been crowded with tourists.

'I mean it!' The man yelled. He held firmly onto Charli, drawing her back so she was in a head lock before he pointed his gun at Logan.

'No!' The word was wrenched from Charli. She forced herself to breathe, to work through this logically. She needed to remain calm. Calm, calm. 'Leave them, Chuck. It's me you want and you have me. They're nothing to do with this.'

He was still edging towards the car. 'You should have thought of that before you started making eyes at lover-boy over there.'

'I'd lost my memory, Chuck. They were helping me find out who I was.'

'Sure, honey.' He didn't believe her and kept his gun

pointed at Logan, who was standing rooted to the spot. 'Stay back.'

Logan couldn't look at the gunman. His eyes were intent on Charli, wishing he'd had the opportunity to say all the things he'd wanted to say. To tell her how much she meant to him and how he felt about her. To tell her that he loved her.

Wil was slowly advancing, talking to the man, trying to get him to see reason, but Logan knew it wouldn't work. Wil was good at his job, but for the moment the bad guy was going to win. A surge of desperation rose within him, knowing Charli was in danger and there was nothing he could do about it.

Once they were in the car and had driven away, Logan would be able to get into his own car and head after them. Although chasing them might not be the best option as the idiot with the gun might crash the car and *then* how could he help Charli? His mind raced, wanting it to be over, trying to figure out his best course of action in a variety of scenarios.

They were at the car now and Logan felt the life drain out of him as he watched the gunman shove Charli across the seat from the driver's side.

The crack of a whip—or a sound like it—punctured the air and Logan watched as the gunman fired at Wil. Another crack pierced the air and he turned to see Wil standing there, his gun drawn. The gunman cried out in pain, his body jerking backwards momentarily. Charli was pushed roughly and fell across the seat.

'Get up. Get up, Charli. Now's your chance.' He said the words, hoping she'd reappear, but she didn't.

Two more shots were fired by the gunman and he heard himself yell 'No!' as he watched Wil crumple to the ground. A squeal of tyres and the smell of burnt rubber filled the air and within another second it was over.

Charli was gone.

CHAPTER NINE

LOGAN forced his legs to move and raced to Wil's side. Next, he forced his brain to work.

'Wil! Wil!' Logan felt for Wil's carotid pulse and thanked God it was there. He looked into his friend's eyes and almost gave in to the sick feeling rising inside him.

'I got shot.' Those three words, mumbled from Wil, were enough to snap Logan out of the entire mind-numbing experience.

'Yes, you did, mate.' He located the area, a few centimetres below the heart, and started unbuttoning his own shirt. He pulled it off and made a pressure pad, holding it down firmly as he wrenched his cellphone from his waistband and dialled Stawell Hospital.

'It's Logan. Wil's been shot in the abdomen. Get an ambulance here, stat. Also, contact Ararat and Stawell police and tell them Dr Charli Summerfield has been kidnapped by an American named Chuck. He's the guy who shot Wil. They left here only a few minutes ago in a dark green BMW convertible, licence plate PSD 888.'

Logan disconnected the call and contacted his mother. 'Go to the surgery and get my emergency medical bag. Wil's been shot.'

'Oh, my word. Is that what that sound was? I thought it was a car backfiring.'

'Well, it wasn't. It was a gun.'

'The kids?'

'They're fine. No doubt shaken, but fine. They're in the store with Mrs Blackwell.' Logan paused, knowing what his mother's next question would be and not wanting her to ask it. She did.

'And Charli? Is she all right?'

'No. He took her, Mum. I don't know what's going to happen.' Logan could feel the panic starting to rise and crushed it immediately. He wouldn't do anyone any good, especially Wil, if he wasn't concentrating. 'I can't think about it now, Mum. I need my emergency bag, oxygen cylinder and a bag of Haemacell, stat.' He disconnected the call and looked down at his friend.

'You hang in there, you hear? Wil?' No response. 'Come on, buddy, open your eyes.' Logan tapped his cheeks. 'William Cecil Fitzgerald—wake up!'

Wil opened his eyes immediately and glared at his friend. 'Don't you *ever* tell anyone my middle name.'

'Then don't doze off or I won't be responsible for *who* I tell. The cavalry are on their way, mate. Hang in there.'

His mother brought his emergency bag and the other things he'd asked for. Logan quickly pulled on a pair of gloves. 'Let's get you stabilised, mate.'

Logan set up the IV line to get the Haemacell started. 'How's your pain?'

'It's OK. I can't feel much of anything.' Wil glanced at him. 'Is that normal?'

Logan nodded. 'Adrenaline's kicked in.'

'Mrs Blackwell's taking the kids to your father.' Rose pulled on a pair of gloves and reached for the sphygmomanometer. 'Hi, there, Wil. How are you doing, love?'

'Not bad, Mrs H.,' Wil said in a strangled voice.

Rose laughed. 'That's the boy I remember. Always making the best of a bad situation. Once we've got you sorted out, I'll give your mum a call to let her know what's happening.'

'Thanks,' Wil said.

'BP's down, respiration and pulse are up,' she announced a little later.

'Keep a close eye on that BP.' Logan pulled a gauze pad from his bag and removed his stained shirt which he'd used earlier. 'The dry-cleaners are going to have fun, getting this out,' he joked, trying to keep the atmosphere light. Wil gave him a weak smile but that was all.

'Where are your kids?'

'They're with my dad. Just relax, mate.'

'And Charli?'

'Let's just concentrate on you for the moment, shall we?' Wil started to close his eyes again and Logan called to him. 'I'll start calling you by your middle name,' he warned, and Wil immediately opened his eyes. 'That's better. Stay with me, mate.' While Logan spoke, he continued to work, ensuring Wil had the best chance of survival.

A group of people had gathered but thankfully Arnold Blackwell was there and was keeping everyone under control and away from what was happening.

'Won't be long now, mate,' Logan said. 'Ambulance is on its way. How's the pain? Feel any pain?'

'Nah. She's right.'

'Good.'

'What about the other guy? What about Charli?'

Logan realised he wasn't going to let it go. 'She's gone.'

'No.' Wil's eyes were wide with confusion. 'But I shot him.'

'From what I could see, I think you got him in the shoulder.'

'He drove off!' Wil's tone hit fever pitch and Rose took his pulse, giving Logan a warning look.

'She'll be fine. The hospital will contact the police in surrounding districts and, I tell you, mate, once they hear that one of their own has been shot, well, you know what you police boys are like. They'll stop at nothing until he's found.'

This news seemed to relax Wil. 'She'll be fine, then.'

'She'll be fine.' Logan repeated the words, hoping that the more he said them, the more he would believe them. He was going out of his mind with worry for Charli, feeling constrained because he couldn't go after them, desperate for his friend as they waited for the ambulance and concerned that his children were all right.

He pigeonholed his thoughts and focused his attention on Wil. Finally, they heard the sound of the ambulance siren. 'Hear that, mate? That's your ride coming.'

'Yeah.' Wil was alert but exhausted and Logan didn't blame him one bit. A minute later, Bruce pulled up and climbed from the ambulance.

'Hey, Wil,' Bruce called as he headed over. 'Looks like you've been having a lot of fun.'

Wil forced a smile. 'Yeah. Logan's been keeping me conscious by blackmailing me.'

Bruce laughed. 'That's what friends are for!'

They transferred Wil to the stretcher and got him into the ambulance. 'How's your pain?' Logan asked.

'Starting to feel it now.'

'Let's give you some morphine to help you out.' Logan looked at his mother as he found what he needed to draw up the pain relief.

'You'll be fine, won't you?' Rose asked.

'Yes. Go and see to the kids. Tell them I love them.'

'I will. What about Charli? What should I tell them?'

Logan looked at his mother. 'Tell them the truth, Mum.'

'But, Logan, they've already been through so much trauma in their young lives.'

'They saw what happened today. Brushing it under the carpet isn't going to do them any favours. They've both developed feelings for Charli and they have the right to know what's going on. Just keep it straightforward and answer their questions in the most direct and easy manner possible.'

Rose nodded. 'All right.' She didn't sound too sure of herself.

'You can do this, Mum. You're a nurse. You've told people bad news time and time again over the years.'

'Yes, but not my own grandchildren!'

Logan smiled. 'You'll do fine. You always do.' He leaned down and kissed her cheek. 'I love you.'

'I love you, too, son.' Tears welled in Rose's eyes as she stepped aside so Bruce could shut the doors.

'Touching,' Wil mumbled. 'Very touching.'

'Keep quiet,' Logan told his friend. 'Just you wait. Within twelve hours—maybe less—your own mother's going to be here, crying over you and kissing you just like she used to when you were little.' Logan administered the morphine and within seconds Wil relaxed.

'Yeah.' Wil smiled. 'Right now, it sounds nice.'

Logan chuckled. 'I'll remind you of that in a day or two.' He kept the banter light, pleased that the Haemacell was doing its job and Wil's vital signs had stabilised.

'How am I doing?'

'Not bad.' Logan unwrapped the pressure cuff from Wil's arm. 'You're in fine shape for an operation.'

Wil looked up at his friend, his gaze intense. 'Who's going to do the operation? Do you trust them?'

'I'm not sure who's rostered on today but I'd trust all of those surgical guys with not only myself but my kids as well.'

'Then I know I'm in good hands,' Wil replied, satisfied with Logan's answer. 'Although I'd still feel better if you could be in the theatre with them. You know, checking up to make sure they don't do anything wrong.'

Logan smiled. 'If it'll make you happy, I'll be there.'

'Thanks.' Wil paused. 'How are you holding up? I mean, about Charli.'

'I'm focusing on you right now.'

'You love her, don't you.' It was a statement but Logan still replied.

'Yes.'

'We'll get her back. We'll find her.'

'*You* just concentrate on getting better.' The ambulance slowed down as it approached the hospital. 'Ready to rock and roll?'

'After you, mate.'

While Wil was off having X-rays taken, Logan was on the phone to the Stawell and Ararat police, giving them as much information as he could. He told them that Charli had suffered from amnesia and didn't have a passport, that Wil had been in contact with the American Consulate. 'Wil shot him in the shoulder so he's bound to be hurt. Besides, if Charli doesn't have a passport, he can't get her out of the country, right?'

'Stranger things have happened,' the cop told him. 'We've sent the information to the police at Tullamarine airport and have put out a call for the car we were told they'd driven off in.'

'Can't you trace the car? He's American. He probably hired

the car. Check with the Melbourne car-hire companies.' He raked his hand through his hair in total frustration.

'That's what we're doing.'

'Wil had information of where Charli's car hire came from. Perhaps it's the same place. Send someone over to his office in Halls Gap to check out his notes.'

'That's being organised as well. Look, Logan, I know you're upset about this—'

'You don't understand—I *love* this woman. I need you to find her.'

'We're doing our best.'

Maree Farnsworth came into the room. 'Logan, he's back from X-ray.'

'I have to go,' Logan growled into the phone. 'Keep me informed.'

'Will do.'

Logan slammed the receiver down and clenched his jaw hard.

'Every muscle in your body is tense,' Maree said softly, and he spun around to face her.

'Wouldn't yours be? She's out there, Maree. Goodness knows what's happening to her. She's been through enough trauma as it is. She doesn't need more. And, to top it all off, my best friend's been shot!'

'I know, but you need calm down.' Maree's tone was firm and to the point. 'Yelling and getting agitated with the police isn't going to solve anything.'

He closed his eyes for a moment and forced himself to take a breath. He slowly counted to ten before opening his eyes and looking at his colleague. 'I hate it when you're right.'

Maree smiled. 'Let's go. Hopefully, by the time you've finished in Theatre, the police will have better news for you.'

'Hopefully,' he repeated, but he couldn't shake the sense of foreboding that was overwhelming him.

It was after five o'clock by the time Wil was wheeled out of Theatre into Recovery. Logan sat with him for a while and once he was satisfied with Wil's prognosis, he stalked to a phone and called the police.

'Logan. How did the surgery go?'

'Wil's doing fine. He'll make a full recovery. What's happening with Charli?'

'We've tracked the car down. It was dumped just outside Ballarat. There was blood on the driver's seat—which fits with you saying the man was shot—but nothing else so far. Also, there was a gun in the car, which we think is the one used to shoot Wil. Forensics are taking both the car and the gun now. We've been in contact with the American Consulate—'

'Have you found her or not?' Logan growled down the phone line.

There was silence for a moment. 'No.'

Logan thumped the desk in anger. 'What about the airport? Have they left the country?'

'Security's pretty tight and, as far as we know, no one matching their descriptions have boarded flights for America.'

'So she could still be in the country?'

'It's possible.'

'But it's also possible they've got out somehow.'

'Logan, this guy seems to have everything planned. He had a car ready to switch, he's left the gun behind, he's covered his tracks.'

Logan shook his head as the fog began to clear. 'This is what she was afraid of. She knew something like this was going to happen. It all makes sense.'

'Run that by me again?'

'Charli was suffering from hysterical amnesia, which means her loss of memory was triggered by an emotional event. She must have something or know something that these people want, and she was running from them.' Logan felt as though one piece after another of the jigsaw was beginning to fall into place. His mind raced ahead, working through different scenarios, and he knew one thing for sure—he'd be able to get things done a lot faster than the police.

'I have to go.' He put the phone down and walked out of the room with a firm, sure stride. He was going to get back the woman he loved and heaven help anyone who tried to stop him!

CHAPTER TEN

THE touch of someone shaking his shoulder made Logan sit up, instantly alert.

'What?'

'Dr Hargraves,' the flight attendant said. 'We're about to land in Los Angeles.'

Logan looked around the plane and remembered where he was. He was on his way to find Charli. The past seventy-two hours hadn't been good to him and he felt as though he'd been running on pure adrenaline the entire time.

Wil was recovering nicely and had his mother fussing over him. 'Feeling cared for?' Logan had teased, making Wil laugh and then complain because it hurt when he laughed. The day after Wil's surgery, the two men had discussed Logan's strategy and his impending trip to the States. When Logan had returned to Halls Gap, he'd made sure his children were all right, patiently answering their questions about Charli and Wil and the entire situation. Then he'd headed to Wil's police office and found copies of the information his friend had gathered on Charli.

As Logan clipped his seat belt into place, he recalled the conversation he'd had with Charli's mother and the light it had shed on the entire situation. Mrs Summerfield had just arrived home after a few days away. She'd won a holiday, which had had to be taken immediately.

. Her mother had been terrified to hear what had happened to Charli. 'Is she all right?'

'I wish I could answer that, but I don't know. She was suffering from amnesia, Mrs Summerfield. We've been trying to get in contact with you for days,' Logan had said.

'And now you're telling me some wild man has kidnapped her? Oh, my poor, dear Charlotte. What's being done? Do the police over there follow up on overseas visitors?'

'Yes, Mrs Summerfield, they do. Can you tell me, was Charli travelling with anyone on her trip to Australia?'

'Oh, let me think. Oh, I'm going all hot and cold. I need to sit down. My poor Charlotte. I hope she's all right.'

'Was she travelling with anyone?' Logan had found it hard to control his impatience.

'Yes. She travelled out there with her boyfriend, Chuck.'

Logan's eyes had narrowed at the information. 'Boyfriend? Are you sure?'

'Oh, yes. They've been together for the past four months now. Before that they worked together. Chuck is a junior vice-president for a large pharmaceutical company. They became very involved on a project of Charlotte's, one that she received funding for. The pharmaceutical company paid for her trip to Australia. All expenses.'

'Do you know what the project is?'

'Oh, I don't go in for any of that technical mumbo-jumbo. That's Charlotte's forté. She's the genius in the family.' Mrs Summerfield choked on a sob. 'Oh, my baby.' She took a breath. 'I have to call the police. I'll have to let them know to do something for my little girl. Oh, dear, it really doesn't make any sense at all. Chuck called me the day I left for my little trip away and said that everything was fine. That Charlotte's conferences had been a big success and that they'd decided to stay a few extra days to do some sightseeing.'

Logan sat up straighter in his chair, the hairs standing up on the back of his neck. 'When did Chuck call you?'

'Um, oh, think, think. I left on Sunday evening—'

'What's Chuck's last name?'

'Fleming.'

'Can you describe him, please?'

'He's a handsome fellow. I know he's going to take good care of my girl.' Logan clenched his teeth at her words but forced himself to keep calm. 'He's about six foot, has sandy-blond hair and grey eyes. I have a picture of them up on my Web site. They make such a cute couple.'

'What's the web address?' She gave it to him and Logan

scribbled it down, reaching over to switch on his computer. 'And you say they've been together for the past four months?'

'Oh, yes. Charlotte was quite taken with him. She's rarely dated at all. Well, you know, she's been so busy with studying and working so I can't really blame her, but Chuck wore her down. He sent her flowers and bottles of wine and all sorts of things to show her his affection and he gave her that lovely gold necklace. I don't think Charlotte was too happy with it, said it wasn't really her style, but she wore it nevertheless. He's a charming man and I can't think of anyone more perfect for my Charlotte. She needs someone to take care of her. Although she's a genius, Dr Hargraves, I'm not short-sighted when it comes to her failings. She's not too good with normal social situations but, then, the true geniuses hardly ever are.'

The Internet was taking its time and Logan's impatience was now at boiling point.

'Oh, dear.' Mrs Summerfield started weeping again and then gave a startled cry.

'What's wrong?'

'Someone's at my door. Oh, my, it's the police. I'd better go, Dr Hargraves. They need to be told everything. Someone has to do something to get my Charlotte back.' She hung up and Logan put his receiver down.

'Someone *is* doing something, Mrs Summerfield,' he growled, as the Web site loaded and a picture of Charli standing next to her kidnapper slowly came onto the screen. Chuck Fleming's arm was about her shoulders and although Charli was smiling, it wasn't a true smile. Not like the ones she'd shared with him.

Regardless of what her relationship had been with Fleming in the past, it was obviously now quite different. The only question was, if she and Fleming were a couple, why had he held her at gunpoint? Logan did a search on the pharmaceutical company Mrs Summerfield had said Fleming worked for. After scrolling through the information, he found what he hoped was the key to this entire traumatic episode.

Charli's research grant for one of her current studies, 'New birth defects caused by the overuse of steroids in pregnant women', was listed there. Charli had briefly touched on it at the conference he'd attended and had announced that she'd be presenting her findings at the international conference in Los Angeles the following week. The conference was scheduled for Wednesday evening. *This* Wednesday evening!

He knew then without a doubt that she had found something, something that wasn't in keeping with the shiny reputation of the pharmaceutical company. Perhaps Fleming had threatened her. That explained why she'd been so agitated when they'd first met. She'd looked over his shoulder and he'd be willing to bet his life that it had been Fleming who had terrified her. Somehow she'd managed to get away from Fleming and had driven to Halls Gap...to find him. The knowledge made him feel special.

It also explained why the hotel had merely said she'd checked out and why her passport and luggage hadn't been found in the room. Fleming had had everything the entire time and Logan knew instantly that, somehow, Fleming had managed to get himself and Charli out of the country.

His stomach lurched as the plane lost altitude and the drive to find Charli and protect her increased once more. As soon as he'd disembarked and gone through immigration formalities, he headed for a phone. He checked in with his parents and spoke to both of the kids. Next, he contacted Stawell Hospital and spoke to Wil.

'I still say you're crazy,' Wil said, his voice echoing down the line.

'That's because you've never been in love.'

'I've been in close contact with the FBI and they're checking the information we've sent over. The fact that Fleming shot a police officer is a big thing to them. Fleming has been formally charged here and we'll seek extradition, but the fact that he's kidnapped Charli and any other violations he's committed since returning to the US will take precedence over our charges. Either way, as soon as they catch up with him, they won't let him walk.'

'First they have to catch up with him.'

'What are you going to do now?'

'I'm going to Charli's research lab. The information she's discovered, which the pharmaceutical company is trying to keep quiet, *must* be there.'

'You're crazy, Logan. Contact the authorities. Agent Smith is the man I've been dealing with. I've given you his number, so use it.'

'I will,' Logan promised.

'I'm worried about you.' Wil's tone was serious. 'You have a family and a life here. Don't go thinking you're a superhero. Those kids of yours have already lost one set of parents.'

'I know. I won't let them down. Take care, mate.'

'You call me every five hours,' Wil demanded.

'I'll do my best.' Logan rang off and carried his hand luggage out of the airport. He hailed a cab and gave the address of Charli's hospital. He had no idea where her lab was and no idea how he was going to get into it, but something would come to him…it just had to.

When he arrived at the hospital, he went to Information and received a map of the facility. He finally found his way to the research building and came face to face with a security checkpoint. 'Here goes nothing,' he mumbled. There was one woman behind the counter and he hoped Charli's statement about his smile being lethal was true. He cleared his throat and smiled.

'Hi. I'm Dr Logan Hargraves and I was hoping to see Dr…' He thought for a moment, as though trying to remember who he was supposed to see. 'Dr Charles Summerfield. That's it.'

The security woman smiled at him. 'You mean Dr *Charlotte* Summerfield.'

Logan frowned. 'I was told the doctor's name was Charlie.'

'It is, but it's short for Charlotte. I'm afraid Dr Summerfield isn't here. Did you have an appointment?'

Logan smothered a yawn. 'I'm sorry. I've just got off a flight from Australia. I wasn't able to see Dr Summerfield on his…er *her*…' he corrected himself '…recent trip to my country, and so a time was set for me to see her this week.'

'Right.' The woman checked the computer and shook her head. 'There's nothing here, but Charli's done this before—

not told us about meetings, that is. For a genius, she can get a little absent-minded at times.'

'I know what it's like.' Logan rolled his eyes. 'I was positive I had a piece of paper here from my secretary, informing me of this appointment, but I have no idea where it's got to.' He patted his coat pockets for emphasis. 'Is her lab assistant available?'

'Of course, Dr Hargraves. I'll ring and ask him to come down.'

Five minutes later, after meeting Charli's lab assistant, Logan found himself standing in her research lab, looking at the Monet painting on the wall.

'Can I get you a cup of coffee, Dr Hargraves?' the assistant asked.

'That'd be beaut. Uh, but I don't drink coffee. Do you have any herbal teas? I've found they're excellent for combating jet-lag.'

'Uh…no, but I believe the doctor downstairs has some. I'll go and get you a cup.'

'Thanks, mate.' Logan counted to ten, then headed over to the Monet. Sure enough, there was a wall safe behind it, with a keypad. 'Believe in yourself,' he mumbled, and took out his cellphone. He checked the numbers against the letters but found that after three numbers the safe gave him an error message. Logan took a breath and thought. 'Believe in yourself.'

He put in the first number corresponding to the first letter in each word but that still didn't work. He frowned. 'Come on, Charli. Help me out here.' He stared at the cellphone once more and remembered the word *yourself* had been shortened to *urself*. He put in 2, 4, 8 for B, I, U, and, like magic, the safe opened. 'You little beauty.' There was one CD in there and he pulled it out, quickly putting it in his bag. 'Why couldn't she just make it easy on herself and remember the three-digit number?' he muttered as he closed the safe.

He'd just put the painting back in place when the lab door opened and a man in a suit walked in.

'Your bandage needs changing again, Chuck.' Charli sat on her chair and looked at the man opposite her, watching as the blood seeped through his crisp white shirt from the dressing beneath.

Chuck looked nonchalantly at his shoulder and shrugged. 'I'll live. Besides, it's just a flesh wound. Country cops are always lousy shots.'

'You're risking infection, not to mention ruining another shirt.'

'How considerate of you. Are you going to change it for me?' His tone was disbelieving. 'I'm not stupid, Charli. If I untie you from that chair, you'll try to escape and then where would I be? Hmm?'

'I wouldn't escape, Chuck. You already have my mother and now Logan.' Charli looked down at the floor, unable to believe Chuck and his goons were holding Logan hostage. They'd shown her a picture of a man, his face battered, bruised and splattered with blood, gagged and tied to a chair. It looked like Logan and her heart lurched.

'If you don't co-operate, we won't be held responsible for our actions,' Chuck had said.

Charli slowly raised her head to glance contemptuously at the man before her. 'You've promised not to hurt them if I co-operate and that's exactly what I'm going to do.'

'What a good girl you are. Nice to see you're being so sensible about this.' Chuck watched her closely. 'I see you're no longer wearing the necklace I gave you.'

'Do you blame me?'

'You really like this hick Australian, don't you?' Chuck continued as though she hadn't spoken.

Charli lifted her chin in defiance, her eyes sparkling with life. 'I love him.' She watched as Chuck's gaze darkened with anger. 'Regardless of what happens tonight at the conference banquet, regardless of what you do to me—or even to Logan for that matter—the truth is that I love him and I always will. I feel for him all the emotions you thought I'd felt for you— but I never did. I can see that now because my love for Logan is real.'

'Oh, how touching. Who cares? You were never anything but an assignment to me and an ice-maiden at that.'

Before her time in Halls Gap, to hear those words from Chuck would have cut her to the quick but now…she felt nothing. Nothing but pity.

The door behind them opened and another man came in, also wearing a suit. He was the only other person she'd seen besides Chuck since the scene in Halls Gap, and it was then she realised that these people weren't hardened criminals, just desperate men, trying to save their jobs and their company.

The man called to him and Chuck went over, the two of them talking in muted tones. Then they turned and looked at her.

'Only a few more hours before we need you to get up to give your speech, Dr Summerfield,' the other man said. 'You obviously can't get up on the podium looking like that so I've arranged for you to have a shower and to change your clothes.'

'Thank you.'

'I trust you won't do anything stupid. We have your friend and your mother. We won't hesitate to hurt them.'

'I believe you.'

'Then we understand each other.' He came to stand beside her chair and took a small key from his pocket.

'Yes.'

He leaned down and undid one side of the handcuffs which had kept her to the chair. He pulled his gun out. 'Let's get you cleaned up.' The man led Charli into an adjoining room, where he removed the other handcuff. 'Clothes are on the bed and there's make-up in the bathroom. You're fifteen storeys up and the windows don't open. The phone's been disconnected and we're right outside the door.'

'I understand.' Once she was left alone, Charli walked on wooden legs to the bathroom and turned on the water. Slowly she undressed, taking off the clothes that had belonged to Trinity's and Owen's mother. As she stepped beneath the soothing spray, every muscle in her body aching from the tension of the past few days, she was thankful Chuck and his associates hadn't linked her with Logan's children. It was bad enough that she'd dragged Logan into it.

She closed her eyes, unable to believe how she'd found herself in such a predicament. The flight back to America had been unbearable as she'd suffered chronic headaches and had eventually been quite sick. She'd read that this sort of reaction was common to amnesia sufferers when their memories returned, but she hadn't expected it to be so violent.

As soon as she'd seen Chuck, her memory had started to return. He had been the trigger for her hysterical amnesia and it had been him who had been needed to snap her out of it again. Yet on the flight visions had swam before her eyes and, combined with the bump to the head she'd received when Chuck had pushed her into the BMW convertible, she'd been unable to control the headache. Chuck had given her paracetamol and codeine and she'd slept for the rest of the journey back to LA.

Now, though, things had settled down…except for her heart which was in complete turmoil. There was no way she could give a false report at the conference banquet tonight but she knew if she didn't do what they'd instructed, Logan would be hurt. Chuck had initially told her back in Australia that if she tried to call the authorities he'd hurt her mother. The fact that she hadn't been able to get hold of her mother had alarmed her, and at the first opportunity she'd fled. She'd driven away from Chuck without a coherent thought in her head—until much later. Then, when she'd seen a sign for the Grampians, she'd remembered Logan.

She closed her eyes. Logan. She prayed they didn't hurt him but she was so torn. She honestly didn't know what to do.

'What would Logan do?' she asked herself, but no answer came.

Logan had said he admired her because she was open and honest. Her time in Halls Gap had been an opportunity for her to really listen to her heart and she knew he was right. She was an honest person and falsifying her results…no matter what the cost to her personally… She couldn't do it.

'Logan.' She whispered his name—her heart, soul and mind aching for him as the tears flowed. And those gorgeous children. Trinity and Owen needed their father. They'd already lost one set of parents.

Logan and the children had shown her a way of life she'd only ever dreamt about and now it was the life she coveted. She wanted to be with them all. She *needed* to be with them all. If only things had happened differently. If only she hadn't agreed to do this research project. If only…

Charli finally managed to pull herself together and finished getting ready. Soon it was time for her to make her appearance at the conference banquet. She walked down the hotel corridor, dressed in a stylish cut navy suit, sensible shoes on her feet and her hair pulled back into her usual chignon. Chuck's arm was close to hers, his gun digging into her side.

'I mean it, Charli. No funny stuff or lover-boy gets it. One phone call. That's all it will take.'

'Is my mother all right? Can you at least tell me that?'

Chuck looked at his colleague, who nodded. 'She's fine.'

Charli nodded, not sure if she should trust the information. 'When did your men take him?'

'What?'

'When did your men take Logan hostage?' They'd entered the ballroom now and Chuck tucked his gun away but kept a firm grip on her arm as they made their way towards the podium.

'About ten minutes after I drove off with you. I couldn't risk him following us so I had my men grab him when he raced back to his house for his car. I told you at the airport that I had him, remember.'

Charli worked hard to keep the frown from her face. What he was saying didn't make any sense. 'I don't remember much about the airport.'

Chuck laughed. 'That's right. You had that bad headache.'

'You shot the policeman, didn't you?'

Chuck's grip intensified and his smile vanished from his face. 'I had to. It was the only way out of there. It doesn't matter. We have your lover-boy, honey, so remember, no funny stuff.'

She was being announced by the other man in the suit, who turned out to be the public representative of the pharmaceutical company. As she mounted the stairs to the podium to a round of applause, Charli knew there was a flaw in Chuck's explanation.

There was no way Logan would have abandoned Wil—or anyone else for that matter—if they'd been critically hurt, just to chase after her. If the bullet had hit Wil, which, according to Chuck, it had, then Logan would have stayed with his friend until he was stable. Logan always did the right thing and it would have been a necessity for him to stay with Wil. Charli shook her head. There was no way they could have grabbed Logan in those circumstances.

She remembered the photographs she'd been shown. The man's face had been battered and bruised, with trickles of blood coming down over his face. The man's colouring was similar to Logan's but was it really him?

She hung her head for a moment and took a deep breath. If she didn't tell the truth tonight, the pharmaceutical company would go ahead, based on the falsified research, and people might die. Her course of action was clear and she raised her head to gaze at the room full of people.

'Good evening,' she said clearly into the microphone. 'Tonight, as stated in your programmes, I'll be presenting the results of my latest research project—'

The doors at the back of the room burst open and a man yelled, 'Stop!'

Everyone turned, people began talking and in complete astonishment Charli watched as a perfectly fit and healthy Logan Hargraves began walking towards the podium, followed by at least a dozen FBI men, all with their guns drawn.

'Where is he, Logan?' Agent Smith asked, and Logan pointed.

'Over there.' Logan pointed to where Chuck was standing at the bottom of the steps, looking frantically around the room for an escape, but Logan knew there wasn't one. Not for him. The man was about to get everything he deserved.

His gaze scanned the room for Charli and he watched as she scrambled in her prim little suit off the edge of the stage and raced towards him.

Both of them darted around tables and people, desperate to reach each other. Just when Charli thought she'd never get there, Logan's arms came around her and his mouth found hers with an urgency she matched.

She'd been in limbo for so long, unsure where she really belonged, but now, being here in his arms, being held close, being cherished by the man she loved, Charli *knew* where she belonged.

Logan pulled back, kissing her cheeks, her eyes, her forehead and finally her lips once more. 'I love you, Charli. I love you so much.'

'Oh, Logan, I love you, too.'

That was all he needed to hear and he crushed her to him once more. The kiss was hot, hungry and highly possessive, and she loved every moment of it. His mouth fitted perfectly with hers, their bodies entwined as close as they could possibly get, and still Logan was nowhere near satisfied.

'You need to marry me.' His breathing was uneven, his tone husky, his eyes desperate and filled with desire.

'Yes. We need to sort this out but, yes. I want nothing more than to be with you for ever.' She touched his face, her fingers trembling. 'They told me they had you. They told me they'd hurt you and they showed me pictures of someone like you who was tied up and beaten and, oh, Logan, I was so scared that I did what they said but then I knew if I didn't tell the truth with my research that lots of people might die and I couldn't do that and I was going to sacrifice you and my mother…' She gasped, her eyes wide with fear. 'My mother? Where is she?'

'She's fine. Fleming sent her on a vacation so you would *think* she was in danger.'

'A…a vacation? You're sure?'

'I've spoken to her myself, Charli. She's fine.' He felt

Charli's body begin to go limp and he held her more tightly against him. He pressed his lips to hers once more to show her everything was going to be all right. 'Let's get out of here.'

'Don't I have to give a statement or something? And what about Chuck?'

They both turned to see Chuck pressed onto the carpet, Agent Smith clamping handcuffs on him. The other man from the pharmaceutical company was also being cuffed.

'The FBI have everything under control for now. I've told them about your research project and have given them the disk containing your *real* data so they could prove it in court.'

'You went to my lab and broke into my safe? How?'

'Well, first of all, I didn't break in. You gave me the combination, remember?'

'Believe in yourself.'

'Yes, and that's exactly what I did. Now, come on. We're not going far.' They made their way through the excited crowd, Logan keeping her firmly by his side. 'Besides, we have other things to discuss first.' He took her to a small room just opposite the ballroom and closed the door. He gathered her close again, unable to believe she was finally here, in his arms.

'The last few days have been...' He broke off, unable to put into words his feelings.

'I know.' She looked up at him. 'Are the children all right?'

'Yes.'

'And Wil? He was shot, wasn't he?'

'Yes. He's doing just fine.' Logan looked around the room and spotted a phone. 'Which reminds me. My five hours is almost up since I last called him and if I don't check in, he's going to bust his stitches.'

Logan took her with him, seating her on his lap and holding her within his embrace as he lifted the receiver and gave the hotel operator the Stawell Hospital phone number. Once Wil was satisfied, Logan called his mother and both he and Charli spoke to the children.

'They love you,' he told Charli once the phone had been put down. He kissed her again. 'So do I.'

'Logan?'

'Yes.'

'There's just one thing I need to check. You've always done things out of necessity. Your children, your life in Halls Gap. They weren't your choices and I just…well, I need to know that you're not…you know, doing this out of necessity.'

He frowned for a moment and raked a hand through his hair. 'Necessity? Yes, of course. Charli, my life in Halls Gap with my children may have *stemmed* from necessity and always doing what was expected of me, but I *love* my life. I was *rescued* by Halls Gap, otherwise I would have ended up a bitter doctor whose only thought was the bottom line.'

'Never.'

'Don't be too sure. Albeit, my change came at too high a cost. I'd give anything to have my brother and sister-in-law back but I've never regretted my move there. How could I? First, it brought me my children and then it brought me you. First my children rescued me and now you're rescuing me by giving me the most precious gift in the world—your love. It was necessary for me to come to the States to find you and it was necessity that spurred me on because *you* are a necessity in my life, Charli. If I don't have you there, I'm only half a person. I need you with me so I can breathe, focus and function properly, because without you…I'm merely a shell. That's exactly how I've felt for the past few days and I don't ever want to feel that way again.' He pressed his mouth to hers, showing her how he felt, knowing his words would be completely inadequate to express the depth of his emotions for her. 'Can't you feel how much I need you?'

'I feel the same.'

He looked up at her and then frowned a little. 'Your memory?'

'All back. As soon as I saw Chuck most of it returned and I realised he was the one I was running from in the first place.' She smiled at him and kissed him. 'And I ran to you because I was attracted to you from the first moment we met and I hoped you were someone I could trust.'

'I'm glad you came looking for me, even if you didn't remember when you eventually found me…or when I found you. Either way, we ended up together.' He kissed her again, unable to control his need. 'I have no idea how we're going to sort everything out—I mean, I can't leave Halls Gap, Charli, and the kids need the stability and—'

It was her turn to silence him with a kiss. 'You talk too much and, besides, I have it all worked out.'

'You do? What is Halls Gap supposed to do with a person as highly accomplished as you?'

'Treat me like a normal person, which everyone there did.'

He thought about that for a moment and nodded. 'I'm sure the hospital would be glad of your services.'

'I'm sure they would but, apart from that, I have another plan.'

'Are you going to tell me or keep me in suspense?' He nibbled at her neck and she giggled, unable to believe she had a right to be this happy.

'Of course I'll tell you. Planet Electronics.'

Logan pulled away and looked at her. 'Planet Electronics! Of course. You said you'd been looking for a company to make a new prototype.'

'Wow, a man who really listens when I talk.' Charli kissed him. 'I thought, when we get back into town, that I'd give your friends there a call and set up a meeting.'

'I'm sure they'd be happy to work with you.'

'I hope so, because if they're serious about branching into the biomedical line in a big way, I'd be the perfect person to manage the project.'

'You're certainly qualified for it.'

'That way, I'm mentally satisfied with work…' She trailed her finger down his cheek and pressed a small, soft kiss to his lips. Logan groaned as burning passion flooded through him at her gentle touch. 'And I'm emotionally satisfied in my home life as wife and mother…' She deepened the kiss, slipped her tongue between his teeth. 'And I'm physically satisfied, being your lover for ever.'

Logan groaned and dragged her closer. 'I've made it a policy never to argue with a woman who's right! Marry me quickly, Charli Summerfield. Be my wife, be a mother to those children who love you so much, be my friend and my lover.'

'Anything you say, Doctor.' And she pressed her lips lovingly to his.

Three months later, Charli walked to the Venus Baths, holding Trinity's hand. Both wore white summer dresses—with twirly skirts, of course—and carried bouquets of native Australian wildflowers. Their hair was free, blowing in the very mild January breeze.

The day was perfect.

She *looked* perfect, Logan thought as he waited impatiently for her to reach his side. He ran a finger around the collar of his shirt and noticed Owen making exactly the same action. He chuckled and squeezed his son's hand as they waited for Charli and Trin to arrive.

'Hurry up,' Owen called as the two women walked slowly and carefully towards them. 'Don't you know it's hot out here?'

Everyone laughed at the five-year-old's impatience, even though Logan silently echoed his son's sentiments. The whole town had turned out to witness the marriage of their doctor to the American woman they'd welcomed into their hearts. Family, friends, locals and tourists. All standing around, smiling in the heat.

In the next instant she was by his side, reaching for him with her free hand, the four of them now joined together.

'Dearly beloved,' the minister began, 'we have come here today to join this...*family* in holy matrimony.'

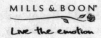

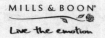

Christmas is a time for miracles...

Christmas Deliveries

Caroline Anderson   Marion Lennox

Sarah Morgan

On sale 3rd December 2004

Available at most branches of WHSmith, Tesco, ASDA, Martins, Borders, Eason, Sainsbury's and all good paperback bookshops.

MILLS & BOON®
Love the emotion

Tender
romance™

THE AUSTRALIAN TYCOON'S PROPOSAL
by Margaret Way *(The Australians)*

Bronte's had enough of rich, ruthless men – she's just escaped marrying one! So she's wary when tycoon Steven Randolph arrives on her doorstep with a business proposal, especially as she finds him impossible to resist. Only then she discovers that Steven is not all he seems…

CHRISTMAS EVE MARRIAGE **by Jessica Hart**

The only thing Thea was looking for on holiday was a little R & R – she didn't expect to find herself roped into being Rhys Kingsford's pretend fiancée! Being around Rhys was exciting, exhilarating…in fact he was everything Thea ever wanted. But back home reality sank in. Perhaps it was just a holiday fling…?

THE DATING RESOLUTION **by Hannah Bernard**

After a series of failed relationships, Hailey's made a resolution: no dating, no flirting, no men for an entire year! But what happens when you're six months in to your no dating year and you meet temptation himself? Jason Halifax is sinfully sexy and lives right next door. What's a girl to do?

THE GAME SHOW BRIDE **by Jackie Braun** *(9 to 5)*

Kelli Walters wants a better life – even if that means participating in a reality TV game show. She has to swap lives and jobs with vice president Sam Maxwell – telling people what to do while he has to scrape by as a single mum! But Sam soon ups the stakes with his heart-stopping smiles and smouldering glances!

On sale 5th November 2004

Available at most branches of WHSmith, Tesco, ASDA, Martins, Borders, Eason, Sainsbury's and all good paperback bookshops.

4 FREE

BOOKS AND A SURPRISE GIFT!

We would like to take this opportunity to thank you for reading this Mills & Boon® book by offering you the chance to take FOUR more specially selected titles from the Medical Romance™ series absolutely FREE! We're also making this offer to introduce you to the benefits of the Reader Service™—

- ★ FREE home delivery
- ★ FREE gifts and competitions
- ★ FREE monthly Newsletter
- ★ Exclusive Reader Service offers
- ★ Books available before they're in the shops

Accepting these FREE books and gift places you under no obligation to buy. you may cancel at any time. even after receiving your free shipment. Simply complete your details below and return the entire page to the address below. You don't even need a stamp!

YES! Please send me 4 free Medical Romance books and a surprise gift. I understand that unless you hear from me. I will receive 6 superb new titles every month for just £2.69 each. postage and packing free. I am under no obligation to purchase any books and may cancel my subscription at any time. The free books and gift will be mine to keep in any case.

M4ZED

Ms/Mrs/Miss/Mr ....Initials ....

BLOCK CAPITALS PLEASE

Surname ....

Address ....

....

....Postcode...................................

Send this whole page to:
UK: FREEPOST CN81, Croydon, CR9 3WZ